MURDER OF THE SAUGATUCK CHURCH BASEMENT KITCHEN LADIES

A Saugatuck Murder Mystery

by

G Corwin Stoppel

Lord Hiltensweiller Press

THE SAUGATUCK MURDER MYSTERY SERIES

ISBN: 9798686594029

Imprint: Independently published

In memory of two great friends –

Bill Galligan and RJ Peterson

Disclaimer

This is a work of fiction.
There is no similarity to any person, dead or alive.

There are a couple of exceptions:
Bobbie, long time-telephone operator;
"RJ" – a mainstay in Saugatuck who has been
around so long I think he might have welcomed the
Butlers when they first arrived in the pioneer days,
and always has the best interests of the city in mind.
And, one of the almost forgotten beloved
eccentrics of our community, "Whistlin' Bill."
Beyond that, the characters are fiction.

Also pure fiction is the murder
itself. It never happened.

As for the buildings and places, for the
most part they're on the up and up.

ACKNOWLEDGEMENTS

*John Thomas who does a wonderful job finding the
typographical error, mangled sentence structure,
and provides some truly beneficial advice.*

*Sally Winthers who creates the covers, puts all
of this together, and makes it possible for you
to enjoy a diversion from today's chaos*

*My wife, Pat Dewey, friend, co-conspirator
in mischief and the joy of living.*

ONE

Even now, decades later, when I recall the night we all had dinner on the deck of the *Aurora*, right after Grandfather and the rest of us had solved the mystery of the murder at Nine Fingers Charlie's Art Emporium, for me it is always "The Night Where Everything Changed – Forever."

For decades, change was, for the most part, good, even wonderful. New experiences, new opportunities, new places to travel and things to do. It was a long upward trajectory of adventures, and I naively believed it would last that way forever. Then came the peak of this lifelong rollercoaster ride, and its descent. Aches and pains, and calendars filled with doctor's appointments. Coffee or lunch with friends became "organ recitals" that had nothing to do with music, and everything to do with body parts that were out of tune. Retirement was another one, and before long eating out all too often meant ham buns, potato chips, and some sort of potato and mustard salad at a funeral reception. I swear I'll come back and haunt anyone who suggests ham buns for my funeral reception. For dessert, either cookies or some sort of Jell-O cottage cheese concoction. Every year Christmas cards were returned, unopened, with the terse notice, "Deceased" written in red ink on the envelope.

All of that was far in the future, and for a while longer, the fun lasted. The Twenties continued to roar and, best of all, I spent even more time with my grandfather.

A night or two after we solved the case of the murder at Nine Fingers Charlie's Art Emporium, we all sat down to a whitefish dinner with baked potatoes, vegetables, and dessert. We were all there

– Uncle Theo and Aunt Clarice, Captain and Mrs. Garwood, Fred, Beatrix, Doctor Landis, and my friend Henry. Mother sat between us to prevent a little discreet handholding under the table. Right after dessert and before we got up, Grandfather rapped his knife against a glass and dropped one bombshell after another. Just as if he was giving a medical report, his voice was flat as he announced he had joined Doctor Landis's practice as a partner, and was moving to Saugatuck. He paused, and then we found out that earlier in the summer Grandfather had bought a vacant lot on the hill. That explained why he had taken such an interest while a new house was being built. Fred was going to move here too and would be living in an apartment over the carriage house. "It'll be nice to be in a house that doesn't roll every time there is a breeze," he told us.

Grandfather had one more big surprise for us. He'd signed over his old paddle-wheeler steamer, the *Aurora,* to the Captain and Mrs. Garwood so they could start a tour boat business. "It's a river boat, and its shallow draft means that the Garwoods can take tourists all the way up river to New Richmond, and maybe further, and then back down again to the lake," he said with triumph. "She was meant for it!"

When he finished, Uncle Theo coughed slightly to clear his throat and get our attention so he could add to the news. He looked a little sheepish as he announced that he and Aunt Clarice were building a summer cottage a few blocks from Grandfather, right across the street from the high school. It was going to be one of those kit homes from Sears Roebuck, just like Grandfather's, where every board was pre-cut and all the hardware was included. A construction crew just had to read the instructions and put it together; or so Sears boasted in their advertisement. They wanted to spend part of the year here, and the winter somewhere warmer. "Probably Florida," Aunt Clarice added, explaining that it was so popular that land prices were going up and up and up.

We were stunned, shocked, taken aback, dazed, and probably a few more things. All I knew is that Grandfather was incredibly generous giving the Garwoods the boat. I couldn't understand why he would give it up, and had to fight back the tears. But then, that was years before RJ and I were sitting in the main room of the Saugatuck Yacht Club, and he told me that a man's happiest day is buying a boat, and his second happiest is when he sells it. I am sure the adage applies to women, as well, even if they didn't mention it. But for me, best of all, I would have Grandfather all to myself. It was probably a little wicked of me, but when Beatrix said she was returning to Minnesota, it was the icing was spread thick on my cake. I knew I'd have to share him with his medical practice, of course, but surgery wasn't as threatening to me as my rival.

With the dinner over and the announcements made, Grandfather stood up and announced it was time to go to Parrish's Drug Store for ice crème.

The next few months were a whirlwind of activity that left my head spinning. Before Grandfather's house was even finished, he started moving things from his cabin on the *Aurora*, including his entire library, up the hill. It wasn't long after that when trucks were at the back door off the alley, and the draymen were carrying in even more furniture. I wanted to see what was happening, but Grandfather said I couldn't come in until he was finished getting the place properly set up. I offered to help move things around, but he was having nothing of it.

At least he showed me his back garden. A couple of hired men were building a fence around the backyard, and he explained that he was going to have flowers planted and have a vegetable garden. That was another surprise because I had never thought of Grandfather as being a gardener; and as it turned out, he wasn't. A few days later a couple of young men came with shovels and rakes, laid out the plots, and turned the soil.

More furniture and crates were carted up the stairs to Fred's apartment. I'll bet the furniture men were confused at the start as to how they were going to get there since there didn't seem to be any stairs. That was because the stairs were on the inside so Fred could park the car and not have to walk up an outside staircase when the weather was bad. That was Grandfather's idea, and it was a good one. By Halloween, Fred was in his apartment.

From the second floor window at the high school history room, I could see the construction crew working on Uncle Theo and Aunt Clarice's home. It was coming along at a steady clip because they wanted to get the cottage framed and enclosed before the cold weather set in. They made it just in time. Finally, on an early November morning, tugboats towed the *Aurora* down the river to where Old Mr. Peterson had his dry dock and boat-works so it could be refitted.

A few days before Armistice Day, Grandfather finally invited Mother and me to see his house. He threw open the front door and ushered us inside with a bow and grand sweep of his left arm, and said with pride, "I decided the time had come to modernize! Enough of that old cluttered Victorian-era decorating from what we had when I was a youngster. From now on, it's going to all be simple, clean lines, and efficiency. And no ferns, either!" I thought what he had done was beautiful. Maybe it was the most beautiful house of all time. Nice oak furniture, a fireplace and a couple of window seats in the living room, he called inglenooks. There were built-in bookshelves in the parlor, and his study looked just like the one he had on his boat, except that he had had a telephone installed, and there was a Victrola with doors in the sound cabinet that opened instead of a big horn. The kitchen was modern, complete with not one, but two zinc sinks, a big black stove and oven, and an icebox. I thought it was the most beautiful house I'd ever seen.

At the top of the walls, there was a six-inch wide strip of wallpaper just below the ceiling, and the rest of the walls were bare plaster painted a light, dull green. "No, I am not putting down carpets. The whole idea is simplicity and economy of effort," Grandfather told Mother when she ask about some rugs. "Now, if you have a spare painting or two I'd be grateful to borrow them. Course, I could always ask....." he let his voice trail away, but I knew what he was thinking. He'd ask Beatrix for a painting.

I loved the house; Mother was not impressed. On the walk home she sputtered and fumed. "Modern, my eye! He's at least twenty years behind the time!" I asked what she meant and she said, "Phoebe, it is all straight-lined minimalist Arts and Craft. Mission Style! The colors for the walls are awful. That went out of style years ago. It's Art Nouveau now – New Art, new architecture, new designs. What did he do, hire the Stickley Brothers as his decorators?

"And that color for the walls! Do you know why he picked that particular color?" she asked, not realizing she was repeating herself. Before I could say anything she answered her own question, "It's the same color used in hospitals, a nauseating green!"

I didn't know who the Stickley Brothers were, but I didn't think they lived in Saugatuck or Douglas. Besides, Grandfather liked it, and if he liked it, then that was all the mattered, and in time Mother calmed down.

After New Year's Day, life settled into a very dull routine. Every morning Mother and I went to school, just like we had been doing for years. On Wednesday, Grandfather and I had dinner together, which never tasted very good because he wasn't much of a cook once he moved beyond sardine on a baked potato. Saturdays, Mother and I cleaned our house and did other chores before Grandfather and Fred came for dinner. Sunday mornings, we either stayed at home or went to the Episcopal church up on the hill.

Grandfather always invited me to come to his house on Sunday afternoons, and he and Fred taught me how to build a fire in the fireplace. Grandfather was wonderful at building a fire. He started with rolling some old newspapers and then twisting them into a knot, and on top of them put some smaller pieces of wood, and finally the logs. On top of that was a little more crumpled-up paper that he lit first. One match was all it took to get a roaring blaze to go. He never lit the paper on the grate because the fire on top would 'draw down' to light the rest of it. "Always take a twist of paper to heat up the chimney, then she'll draw right from the start," he would always remind me, even when I was allowed to do it.

We didn't talk much on Sunday afternoon; we read. One afternoon I asked him just two questions – why he didn't go to church anymore, and if he knew who was building the house behind him. He told me he had no idea about who was building a house. As for going to church, he thought there was too much doctrine in most churches.

We were like the groundhog – still waiting for spring, even if we saw our shadow. Very early in March, Grandfather came out of hibernation. I'd been reading in his library and finished a book. When I went to return it to the shelf I started looking for something new and came across a book by a doctor named Sigmund Freud. I'd been reading it for about an hour, well, *trying*, to read and understand it when Grandfather saw me.

He came out of his chair, snatched the book away, and said I wasn't old enough to be reading that sort of thing. I blurted out, "But I want to become a doctor, just like you." He turned around slowly and looked at me so intensely I thought I was in trouble.

"You do?" he asked.

"Yes," I could barely whisper. "If it is all right with you, and you don't mind."

His face froze for a moment, and then he smiled. After that, nothing was ever really the same again. In an instant, our lives changed directions. It was almost as if I had suddenly grown up in his mind, and he started treating me more and more as an adult! Before long we were having serious, grown up, conversations. I sometimes wondered if he forgot I was still in school and not a medical student or intern. That's because he gave me his desk copy of *Grey's Anatomy*.

I realized that our lives really had changed the Sunday afternoon when Grandfather was helping me memorize the Catechism so I could be confirmed when the bishop came to Saugatuck sometime in the early summer. We were reviewing what I had memorized the previous Sundays, and then he paused. He pulled out his pipe and slowly filled it, and struck a match. I knew that meant he was stalling for time before he told me, "You know, I approve of you doing this, but we need to talk. Helping you with your studies has made me realize there is a dangerous similarity between the worst of medicine and religion."

"What do you mean?" I asked.

"If you are going to be a physician, you need to think about this, Phoebe. You might as well start now. Now, you already know about the founder, the father, in a sense, of medicine, Hippocrates. He said the first rule of medicine was to do no harm. Phoebe, you've had some friends from school who have had their appendix removed, haven't you?"

"Yes," I answered tentatively.

"Do you know what happens if the appendix becomes infected and ruptures? Generally, a person dies from blood poisoning. Back when I was your age, that's what often happened, and it was a miserable way to go. It happened to some boys I knew in school, and they were practically screaming in pain until they passed away. Then surgeons began cutting into the abdomen and removing the appendix, and the patient usually lived. Now, you tell me, is that a good or bad thing?"

"It's a good thing!" I answered quickly.

"Yes, and I agree, and so would old Hippocrates, so today we remove the appendix. It's the standard treatment. Now, here's the challenge: Early on, some professors of religion said it was a bad thing because we surgeons were playing God. In other words, they had a belief, a doctrine, that God appoints a time for a person to die. They said we were doing a bad thing because we are interrupting God's plan for that person."

"Do you mean it was your beliefs against their beliefs?" I asked tentatively.

"That about sums it up. Two different conflicting sets of beliefs and two opposing doctrines, but remember, not everyone got into the fray over this. I'd say it is what happens just about any time there is a new invention or an idea. It goes against someone's beliefs of what is right.

"The problem with doctrine, at least the way I see it, is that if the fellow who came up with that idea can convince a couple others to go along with it, and they get others to agree with them, then suddenly it becomes a doctrine. And it doesn't matter if it is true or false. It's practically carved into stone. It doesn't matter whether it's medical, religious, or almost anything else. It includes art and music, too. Do you understand?"

"I think so," I said, still trying to figure it out. "What are you trying to tell me?"

"Just this: Think for yourself and always have an open mind and don't be afraid of asking questions. Lots of questions. You know which question is the most important one?"

"No," I said.

"Why. W-h-y," he spelled it out. "That's the important one. Always ask why someone believes something or why they're doing something. That's how you'll learn the most. Now, keep that in mind and let's move onto the next question Just look at everything in the world and ask why someone thinks you should know it and why you should believe it. Ask why they believe it and do it. And remember, nothing is more important for a future doctor than to have an inquiring mind and never, ever, fear curiosity."

Only later did I realize that was one of the most important twenty minutes of my life.

I was so interested in what he just taught me I almost forgot all about my second question. Then I remembered. I'd been watching the construction of the new house behind Grandfather's and asked him if he had found out who owned it. I watched as he slowly pulled out the knife on his watch chain, took a long time scraping the bowl of his pipe, then folding the blade and putting it back in his pocket. It took him such a long time I knew meant it was going to be bad news, and he was trying to figure out the best way to tell me.

"Well now, as you know, Doctor Landis and I enlarged our laboratory and we hired a pathologist on a part time basis," he said.

"Beatrix?" I could barely whisper. "Doctor Howell?" I corrected myself.

"That's right. She's probably one of the best in the country. We're fortunate to have her because it means we can give better care to our patients," he said after he relit his pipe for the third time. "And, it will be good for her. You know, she's getting older, too, and she wants to do more painting. She'll be close to Ox-Bow, and she's got a studio with northern lighting, just like Monet had in his studio. I met him once when I was in Paris. I'll tell you about it one of these days. Plus, if she gets a commission to research a painting, she can take the train into Chicago and go anywhere in the country. Not bad, eh?"

I let out a deep sigh. Not bad for her, maybe, but I knew I wasn't going to have Grandfather all to myself anymore.

Sure enough, once she moved and got settled in, Mother felt duty-bound to invite her to our weekly dinners.

Things change.

— Dr. Phoebe Walters

TWO

"Thunderation! Putting together this ribbon cutting for the lab is more work than building the blasted thing!" Horace growled at Beatrix and Doctor Landis.

"What do you mean, Horace" she asked.

"We finally got the mayors of Saugatuck and Douglas to be present on the 11th of next month, but now the director the high school band isn't certain about the date because they're on summer vacation. The masons are in a snit because we don't have a cornerstone for them to lay, and want to know why we can't have the contractors come back here to make room for one. Thunderation! It's a wooden frame building! And then, the Odd Fellows have some big palaver in Midland that day so they'd like us to pick another date. As if that isn't enough, there are these!" Horace held up half a dozen letters.

"What are they?" Doctor Landis asked.

"Letters from four local ministers, all wanting to give the invocation or preach a sermon. Or both They say they wrote *merely* to offer their services, but they want to be the chosen one. I'll be you everyone of them will start off with a prayer that mutates straight into some long-winded sermon telling the Almighty what He already knows and instructing him on what He ought to do.

"And then there are these letters," Horace said, holding up another small stack. "Letters from the ladies aid committees from all of the churches, begging, no, practically insisting that they should be the ones to do the decorations and refreshments. Listen to this one. 'Our members are renowned for their nice, interesting little cookies.' What in thunderation is a nice little cookie? How is it different from a not-nice cookie? Or are little cookies somehow better than big ones? What makes them so interesting?

"Or this one telling me that the rules of their church don't allow their members to drink booze, play cards, dance, smoke or anything else which means they are all healthy. And since a hospital promotes health and they promote health, they want to do the refreshments. What in the world does that have to do with anything?"

"Well, just pick one preacher and pick a different church. It isn't that difficult," Doctor Landis suggested.

Horace was about to agree with him when he noticed Beatrix was staring into the distance, thinking. He paused to give her time.

"There may be a better way. Instead of having one of the clergymen give the invocation, perhaps you could prevail upon Phoebe to do it. Surely, no one could object to having a young layperson, a woman, do it, especially if it is your granddaughter," Beatrix said quietly, still looking out the window.

"I agree," Horace said quickly. "Or Landis, what about one of your boys? Or, all three of the youngsters."

"I'll ask the boys, but they're at the age where standing in front of a bunch of people and praying won't be an easy sell," Doctor Landis answered. "Still, the good thing is they'll keep it short."

"As for the decorations and refreshments, instead of asking any one of the churches, perhaps it would be better to ask the Saugatuck Garden and Tea Society to do it," Beatrix continued.

"Why?" Horace wanted to know. "And who are they?"

"A women's group here in town that like flowers and tea," Landis said, interrupting Beatrix.

She continued. "If you ask any one church group to do it, the others will have their noses out of joint. They will hold it against you for years. People in small towns have memories that last for generations, especially the bad ones. If you ask them to all work together, it is very likely that their rivalries will get the best of them and then you will be patching up knife wounds, fractured skulls, gouges, and bruises. But, many of the tea ladies belong to a church, although I know that may not be true of all. The women will work together under a bigger umbrella. Of course, I do not mean a literal umbrella. A better choice of words would have been 'auspices.' They will work together under the auspices of an outside group."

"Why should they be nicer if we do it that way?" Doctor Landis asked.

"For the same reason that if you invite a guest to dinner then everyone in your home will be on their best behavior. I have often been invited for that reason, not for my sparkling wit and personality. The same thing should happen with the tea party ladies," she told them.

"She's right. My boys mind their p's and q's when you come over, Horace," Landis added.

Both Horace and Doctor Landis stared at Beatrix. "Give her the Wisdom of Solomon Award for the year," Horace said. "That should take care of matters, and take the heat off us. With that, we can announce the date – the 11th. And all we have to do is be there, smile a lot, and say 'thank you' to everyone."

On the day of the grand opening, Horace did his best to remain patient and smiling, even if it did take a few reminders from Beatrix and Phoebe. The crisis was what he was to wear for the event. "It's after Decoration Day, so I'll wear my white suit," he told Harriet. She was afraid it might look too informal, so he countered with his black suit. Phoebe thought he would look like a funeral director and send the wrong visual message. "Boss, say, why don't we wear our uniforms? No one could object to that."

"Thunderation! Anything for some peace and quiet! Uniforms. Dress uniforms. Order of the day, Sergeant!"

Fred had the good sense not to tell Horace that their Army uniforms had originally been Beatrix's idea passed on to him.

The American Legion Color Guard led the parade, with the three doctors following. Dr. Landis's boys and Phoebe filled out the third rank, with the two village mayors right behind them. Behind them was the high school band, surprising a few parents when they marched in step and all played the same tune at the same tempo. Right behind them were the top hat-wearing former Grand Masters from the Masonic Lodge, a delegation of Noble Grands from the Odd Fellows who came back early from their meeting in Midland, and members of the Knights of Pythias, Woodsmen of the World, plus half a dozen women who had their allegiance with the Maccabees. "I'm half surprised there's anyone left in town to watch the parade," Horace whispered to Phoebe when they took their places atop the front steps of the hospital.

"Saugatuck loves a parade, any parade," she whispered back

A reporter from the Commercial Record took notes as Phoebe stepped up to the megaphone and gave a forty-two second long invocation. The mayor of Saugatuck spoke for about two minutes, and not to be outdone, the mayor of Douglas, who was up for re-election in the fall, held forth for a good ten minutes until he realized the crowd was getting restless and he needed to quit before he put the voters to sleep. Finally, Doctor Landis was able to produce an oversized pair of scissors so that he, Beatrix, and Horace could cut the ribbon. They froze in place so a photographer with the newspaper, complete with flash powder, despite the sunny afternoon, could take a picture.

"Thank you all for coming, and now, a big thank you to the Garden and Tea Society for organizing the decorations and refreshments," Doctor Landis added. He stepped back from the megaphone and whispered to Horace and Beatrix, "And now we'll do a bit of glad-handing. Come on, you two."

"I think I'll slip off to Parrish's for a Green River," Horace said with a straight face.

"Horace, for once I agree with your idea of a Green River, as long as I can have almost anything else," Beatrix said with a slight smile.

"No such luck, you two. You're staying put at least for half an hour. It won't kill you, you know," Doctor Landis insisted. "Come along children, or daddy is going to give you a good spanking for misbehaving."

"Thunderation!" Horace growled under his breath.

"I heard that," Doctor Landis told him.

Working the crowd turned out far better than Horace and Beatrix expected. A young man, Andrew Clarke, came loping across to them and introduced himself. "I'm the new town police chief, and I thought this might be a good place to find you and meet you, he said, pumping Horace's right hand, then turning to Beatrix. "Sure am glad to meet you both!"

"New chief, eh?" Horace asked. "I didn't know that Chief Garrison was gone."

"He left a month ago, Horace," Beatrix told him.

"I didn't know that. I've been a bit busy," Horace said quietly.

"I know you folks are busy right now, but maybe sometime we can have coffee and donuts so we can get to know each other. The way I see it, the town doctors and police ought to try working hand in glove."

Horace smiled broadly. "I like the way you think. I agree. We'll get together in a couple of days."

"He is a nice young man, is he not?" Beatrix asked when the chief had moved on to greet others. She looked over her shoulder as he left.

Eight days later Miss Stymington's body was found on the floor in the basement kitchen of her church, the Congregation of the Heavenly Blessed.

It was a little after ten on a Monday morning when Myrtle DeLuca, the secretary, opened the back door to the church, hoping for a quiet day in her office. Her first order of business was to make a pot of coffee for herself, half-hoping she wouldn't have to share it. She walked down to the kitchen as always, turned on the lights, and sucked in her breath as she said, "Oh dear." There on the floor was Miss Stymington. Later that morning, when the chief interviewed her, Mrs. DeLuca repeated her initial words, then said she had not touched a thing, backed out of the kitchen, ran back upstairs and called him from her desk.

The chief took an officer with him, and after making a preliminary investigation of the deceased and the kitchen, called the hospital.

"I'll be right there," Horace told him.

"No, stay there. I'm coming to get you," the chief said urgently.

Horace turned to Luella Clawson, the hospital secretary and asked her to put a call through to Doctor Howell. "Tell her we'll be right there to get her. Black bag time. Tell her that. Those words: Black bag time. She'll know what it means."

"I don't want to interfere with your business, but I assume you left someone to watch over the deceased and secured the room," Horace said as he got into the police car. "We need to pick up Doctor Howell. She ought to be outside by the time we get to her place."

"Yup. I got one of my men there now. At the church, that is. And before you ask, I checked both her wrist and her neck for a pulse, and there wasn't nothing. I even had the secretary to give me her compact so I could hold it up to the deceased's lips to see if she was breathing. Nothing.

"Now, the reason I came to get you is that there's something you ought to know. This is my first death call. I mean, I've seen dead bodies before and all, but not as a policeman where I have to investigate it. I'd appreciate it if you wouldn't say anything about it to the other fellows, but I thought you ought to know. See, I might need some advice on, well, how to proceed, what to do next, and that sort of thing. What I'm trying to say is I want to do the investigation the right way, and I'm sort of turned around, if you get my drift."

"All right. We'll make sure we tell you everything we're doing and everything we're thinking as we go along. That should help. And we'll keep your secret to ourselves."

"Thanks. I figured telling you was the smart thing to do so I don't make too many mistakes," Chief Clarke said.

"You're right on the money on that one."

"Much appreciated, Doc. Say, there's something I ought to ask you, strictly for professional reasons, because I don't really care one way or the other. You and Doctor Howell. I've heard you two work together, but...."

Horace smiled. "If you're going the long way around the mulberry bush to ask if there's more to our relationship than a professional one, the answer is 'no.' We've known each other half a century. We're friends, and that's it, and we want to stay friends, so that's the way we want to keep it."

"Understood. I just didn't want to put my foot in my mouth," the chief said.

Horace quickly turned the conversation. "Now look, if you're worried you might not be perfect, worrying is a good thing sometimes. Keeps you on your toes! Thunderation, the first time I held a scalpel in my hands I was scared stiff. And that was on a cadaver, not a living, breathing patient. Still feel the same way now when I'm washed up and the nurse puts the scalpel in my hand. The deceased isn't going anywhere, and Doctor Howell and I will be doing the autopsy, so you're job is primarily to collect any evidence. And then take a statement from anyone who saw and heard anything. Besides, more likely than not, it is probably natural causes. Don't forget, she was an older woman." The chief slowly pulled to a stop.

"One other thing, Chief. This is a death call. Try not to prejudice your mind by seeing things that aren't there, missing something, or jumping to a conclusion. My advice is to treat it as a routine death call."

"I've never ridden in the back seat of a police car before," Beatrix said flatly as she opened the rear door to step in.

"I suspect you'll find it a highly over-rated experience," Horace told her. "That blue dress looks new....?" He asked.

"Yes, Horace. Brand new. A Christmas present to myself to celebrate the end of the Great War. The same brand new blue dress I wore last week." He could tell she was irritated with him.

"Let's get out of the kitchen and give the chief time to examine the floor for any evidence before we trample through," Horace suggested to Beatrix once they had examined Miss Stymington for any sign of life. They stepped back to make room for the chief, and when Horace turned toward Beatrix he ran his index finger along the side of his nose and silently mouthed the words, "First time." She nodded to let him know she understood.

They watched as the chief slowly worked his way through the kitchen, crawling carefully and slowly on his hands and knees, looking under the counter, the stove and icebox, and the sink. "There doesn't seem to be anything out of the ordinary. I'm ready to release the body," he told them.

Beatrix disagreed and cautiously suggested, "Perhaps not. This is something I am forever reminding the interns and residents, and sometimes even experienced surgeons such as Doctor Balfour. Now that you have not found anything unusual, search again, this time for something that is missing that should be present. That is sometimes much more challenging."

While the chief searched the kitchen for a second time, Beatrix focused on the deceased. "I am certain you noted the flushed face," she whispered to Horace. He nodded in acknowledgement. "I think this warrants further investigation," she told him. "Can you or the chief arrange to transport the body to the hospital? Before that is done, I think it would be wise to examine her handbag in the chief's presence for any possible evidence."

"Are you suspicious of something?" Horace asked.

Beatrix didn't answer.

MURDER OF THE SAUGATUCK CHURCH BASEMENT KITCHEN LADIES

THREE

"It appears to me to be a massive heart attack, but I'll defer to you," Horace told Beatrix once they returned to the hospital and prepared for the autopsy.

"Possibly," she said cautiously and without enthusiasm. "Let us not rush forward. When we first arrived at the church, she presented with considerable flushing on her cheeks. It has faded now, so we can rule out too much habitual alcohol use that would have broken the small capillaries on her cheeks. There is some bruising near the right temple, but that could be from when she fell, perhaps hitting her head on the counter, or more likely, on the floor. Both earrings are in place, so perhaps she collapsed slowly. Pearls are the mark of a more affluent woman; very nice. We will keep that information for future reference. First, we examine the shoes. Always start with the shoes because they reveal many deep secrets."

Beatrix pulled hard on the left shoe, finally getting it off Miss Stymington's foot. As she held it up to the light she told Horace. "Sensible shoes, are they not? There is nothing frivolous about them. Notice that they have been recently cleaned and polished. Not even a scuff mark on the uppers on the left one where she might have brushed against the right. No organic or other foreign material on the soles. In short, a fastidious woman. I wish I had taken the opportunity to know her better. She was methodical, self-assured, and had absolute confidence in her strengths."

"All that from her shoes?" Horace asked.

"Yes," Beatrix said quietly. She looked at the heels of both shoes. "We can also conclude that she does not have any spinal problems.

Both shoes are evenly worn. And, I might add, sensible cotton stockings as well. Cotton, not silk. Now, this is interesting. She was a thrifty woman."

"Beatrix, how can you come up with that conclusion?" Horace asked in exasperation.

"She wore a hole in the toe of her left stocking and it is darned. A spendthrift would merely have thrown it away."

Horace let out a low whistle.

"Now we are ready for the head." Beatrix stood to one side and looked closely at the crown of her head. To his surprise, she giggled. "Oh, this is interesting! The color of her hair is not natural. Look closely, Horace, and you will see her natural color is grey. She had her hair dyed about a week ago." Beatrix giggled again. She pushed a lock of hair away with forceps.

"And why is that important?" Horace asked.

"There are three reasons a woman her age would dye her hair. The first would be to make herself look more attractive to a male. As long as I have known her or about her, she has never been known to have mentioned a beau, and neither have any of her friends spoken of it. So, we must see if there was one in the recent past. A jilted suitor or someone with whom she attempted a reconnection. If it is foul play, that will be a task for our police chief. Second, a woman dyes her hair for other women. She wants to look better than the others in her social set, or to look stronger and more healthy. From what I heard from Harriet several weeks ago, Miss Stymington had considerable clout in the Garden and Tea Society, the woman's club, the photography club, as well as her church and played bridge at least two afternoons a week. In short, she saw herself as something of the queen bee, which meant she used the appearance of her hair to help retain her position. Appearance is power, and for some, power is everything. It is a pity that Clarice is not here. We could ask her about her knowledge of the deceased."

"That's two reasons. What's the third?" Horace asked.

Beatrix looked up at him. "Why, for herself, of course," and then winked. "And no, I do not. Now, please stay focused."

"There is a bit of liquid on the inside of the left ear. Wax, perhaps?" Horace observed.

"Do not touch it, and do not let her head move. Please hold it very steady." Beatrix said. She went to the cabinet and found an eyedropper and swabs. As she began collecting the liquid she whispered to herself, "There is not very much, and it is not wax." To Horace she said, "Let me try again." She made a second attempt and held up the eyedropper in triumph, and handed it to Horace. "There isn't much to collect, but it should be sufficient. It may be nothing more than water from her morning ablutions. Still, we must find out. Hold it upright, please." She put the swabs into a glass petri dish and put the cover in place. The eyedropper was placed, inverted, onto a test-tube holder.

"And now for the main event," Beatrix said cheerfully as she reached for a scalpel. Horace, man the rib spreaders, please,"

For a few minutes they worked in silence, glancing up at each other every few seconds to make sure their efforts were coordinated, as she opened the deceased's chest and Horace turned the ratchet to spread the deceased woman's ribs. "Glad you have small hands, Doctor. Either I'm getting old and weak or she was a tough old bird," he said. She ignored him.

"Fascinating," Beatrix said as she raised the heart into view. "The victim presents with the appearance of a severe heart attack, and yet there is no indication of a blockage. Nor is there scar tissue from any previous heart damage. There is little more to see here," she said after five minutes. She pushed the heart back into the chest cavity. "You might as well close." Beatrix stared at the opposite wall, silent and unmoving, while Horace released the spreader.

"There is an ontoscope in the second drawer of the middle cabinet," Horace said, as he continued to close the incision.

"What led you to say that, Horace?" Beatrix asked.

"Because I know your methods. You were intrigued by the liquid in her ear, we looked at her heart and found nothing out of the ordinary, you have been thinking and by now you have an idea. That idea will require you to examine her ear again."

"Yes, you are very right. Thank you," she answered flatly. "Good work, Sherlock. I will return presently and we will continue the examinations."

When Beatrix returned to the examination table, she handed Horace the device. "Please look very carefully. I suspect it will be difficult to see if the ear drum has been perforated."

"And...?" Horace asked an open-ended question.

"I will be taking the samples to the lab to see if my theory is correct," she said.

They met in the hallway, Beatrix walking back to the examination room, Horace about to enter the laboratory. "You were right, the eardrum was perforated. What about you? What did you find?" Horace asked.

"As I suspected: The liquid is digitalis. I did two tests. The first was barium peroxide; the second, paracetric. Both results were the same. Digitalis. There is no doubt in my mind. A sufficiently large dose to be fatal. From what you just told me, it appears the digitalis was injected through the eardrum, absorbed into her system, and that is why we recovered such a small amount That makes this a murder case."

"No, Beatrix. It is a pre-meditated murder case. If she had been frightened, pushed, even hit by a blunt kitchen object it would have been murder; but for someone to carry a hypodermic needle with a strong poison and then inject it into the ear, that makes it pre-meditated murder. Whoever did this went to the church with the intention of killing her."

At first, Beatrix said nothing. "I believe the choice of the eardrum was cunning and intentional. No puncture wound on the body. Clever. Our new police chief will have quite the challenge for his first case." She was smiling as she pulled the mask off her face. "We had best telephone Chief Clarke. While we wait for his arrival I suggest we make a small incision through the ear drum and retrieve any additional digitalis."

"You really *are* enjoying this, aren't you? You do realize that the chief is already in over his head. It isn't the chief who'll be solving this. It's you and I," Horace reminded her.

"Yes. I know it is wicked, but I do like a challenge. The killer is very devious. I suggest you place the call while I continue with the examination," she told him.

Horace pulled off his gown, gloves, and mask before going to his office to place the call. "You sitting down, Chief? Sorry to interrupt you. This is Doctor Horace Balfour. Doctor Howell and I are still here at the hospital. Here's the gist of it. The deceased, Miss Stymington, appears to have been murdered. I think you ought to come over here right away. One other thing, and I know it is not my place to tell you what to do, but it might not hurt to have a second set of eyes go over the church again. Not just the kitchen, but the whole building and grounds. Tell whoever does it to be careful because they're looking for a hypodermic needle with poison."

There was a long silence, and Horace asked, "Chief, you still there?"

"Yeah, just taking it all in. That, that, well, it came as a surprise. I'll send a man over to the church, and I'm on my way over to the hospital. See you in a couple of minutes."

The chief looked like a raccoon caught when the front porch lights come on unexpectedly. "You two are serious, aren't you?" he asked. They nodded that they were. "Back in college there were a couple of fellows who liked to razz the freshmen." He looked at their stony faces, shook his head, and said quietly, "But you're serious."

For the next few minutes Horace and Beatrix carefully explained every detail of their work during the autopsy. "If Doctor Balfour had not noticed a very small amount of liquid in her ear we would have declared this a death by natural causes," Beatrix said. "I have preserved the samples and tests for you as evidence."

"You sure it isn't just plain old rat poison or something like that?" the chief asked.

"No. Digitalis. A very potent poison used to speed up the heart," Beatrix answered.

"I've never heard of something like this," Chief Clarke said. "You have anything more for me?"

"Not yet. We're finished here and I think you can call the undertaker to make the arrangements. Look, we're going back to my place to write our reports. You'll either find us there or I'll call you."

The chief quietly said, "I'll call you when I can."

MURDER OF THE SAUGATUCK CHURCH BASEMENT KITCHEN LADIES

FOUR

Horace and Beatrix spent the late morning and most of the afternoon in Horace's library, writing their medical report for Chief Clarke, carefully going over every word to make certain it was accurate and clear. "All things considered," Horace observed, "I can't help but wonder if we should write an explanation in laymen's terms for him. It's that or we'll have to translate parts of it for him."

"He is inexperienced, is he not?" Beatrix agreed. "Yes, not parts. All of it. Perhaps we should go for a short walk, just around the block, to rejuvenate the brain."

When they returned they spent another hour working on a second document, finally agreeing that their work was finished. Beatrix was staring at the wall opposite from where she was sitting, obviously thinking about something. "Horace," she finally asked, yawning at the same time "do you think we are drawn to murder, like Chief Garrison once said? That troubles me. I am very sure that your brother thinks much the same thing of us."

She had asked the question many times, and each time he had to reassure her. "Oh, I don't think we are. We're both physicians, so death is part of our work, our life. Most of the time it is from natural causes, but then again, there are times like this. I think murder seems to be drawn to us, not the other way around. I mean, we don't go out looking for it, now do we? No business cards, no two inch advertisements in the paper. No, it just happens."

"No. Very likely you are correct. Thank you. That was re-assuring. I did not want to take pleasure in it."

Both of them were startled to hear a knock at the study door, and before either of them could answer it, Harriet and Phoebe came in. "I just heard Miss Symington passed away," Harriet began.

"Yes. This morning," Horace told her, hoping not to be asked for more information.

"From the cigar and pipe smoke in this room, I suspect you found another nice juicy murder!" Phoebe said brightly.

"Phoebe!" all three adults said in unison. "That is not the proper thing to say," her mother added. "It's not nice; it's morbid and it is very wicked of you!" Turning to Horace and Beatrix she asked, "Well?"

"Murder," Beatrix said distantly. "We suspect it might be premeditated murder."

Horace cleared his throat and looked at his granddaughter. "Just in time to help out on the case, Phoebs. How about you taking this report down to Chief Clarke for us? He needs it right away." He handed her the report inside a file folder. "And no peaking; this is police business; official police business, understood? It's for his eyes only." He looked at her, slightly lowering his left eye-lid.

The girl was delighted. She would be working with her grandfather again. Even better, he was letting her know the inside information. "Mother, may I borrow your car?"

"Yes," Harriet said reluctantly. "Right down there and then right back here. The keys are in the starter. No wandering off somewhere, and no boys!"

"Some day, Harriet, someone is going to borrow your car without asking. You really shouldn't make it so easy for them. Why don't you put the keys in your handbag when you get out?" Horace suggested.

"Horace! This is not the big city. People don't steal cars around here. It would almost be like saying I don't trust people if I always took out the keys. What would people think of me? The next thing and we'll be locking our doors."

He smiled, not wanting to remind her that she did lock their doors when they were gone from home. The key was over the door jam.

As soon as Phoebe was out the door, Harriet pulled her chair closer to the others, looked over her shoulder to be certain her daughter was gone, sat down, and eagerly asked, "Okay! Tell me what happened to her!"

"Harriet! Thunderation! You're as bad as Phoebe," Horace chided her. "The simple story is she was found dead on the floor of the basement kitchen at the Church of the Heavenly Blessed," Horace said. A glance at Beatrix, and he understood that they were agreed they were not going to say anything more.

Harriet gasped, "That's terrible. She was so involved in her church and in the community. Garden and Tea Club, camera club, the Hawthorn Reading Group, her church... Well, I just said that, camera club, bicycle club, literary club, art club, everything!"

"She will be missed," Horace replied. "She must have been well liked..."

"Well...," Harriet said, not finishing her sentence. The tone of her voice made it clear – not everyone appreciated her.

"A little pushy?" Horace asked.

"Well, more like very pushy at times. Most of the time, in fact. She always had to be in charge, the queen bee." Harriet noticed Beatrix's eyebrows rise. Only a few hours earlier Beatrix had proposed the same thing. Now it was confirmed.

"Reminds me a bit of the late Fairy Nightshade," Horace stifled a chortle.

"No, Fairy Nightshade was a vicious blackmailer, ruthless, with an odious personality. Miss Stymington was different. She was one of those women who knew how to get things done, and pushed hard. She rubbed people the wrong day," Harriet said.

"I cannot say that I am surprised to hear that, Harriet. Many times people, especially women, who assume leadership, are not fully appreciated," Horace said. "Right, Beatrix?" She nodded in agreement.

"It is sometimes even truer when a woman has the reputation of being one who can get things done," Beatrix told them.

While Phoebe was away on her errand, Harriet, Horace, and Beatrix talked about Miss Stymington. The more Harriet told them, the more obvious it became that she was involved in every social committee in the village; at least the important ones. But that still didn't mean she was popular. Horace and Beatrix were getting a clear picture of her personality. She had a way of controlling people that set them off. She was pushy and had a talent for raising the hackles on others.

Phoebe knew it was not right to look at the file folder that her grandfather and Beatrix had asked her to deliver to the chief, even if Horace had given a half-wink. Still, if Miss Symington was unexpectedly dead, and her grandfather and Beatrix were writing a medical report at his home, it could only mean one thing – murder. As far as Phoebe was concerned, murder meant a new adventure to be shared with her grandfather. She found a parking space on Butler Street, looked around to see if anyone were near, and with the folder flat on the car seat, quickly opened it and scanned through the pages. She could make her way through most of the document without difficulty, except for some of the medical terms. But it was the last three words that caught her attention: "conclusion: premeditated murder". She was right. It *was* murder! She sucked in her breath to compose herself, then closed the folder and took it to the chief.

"Doctor Horace Balfour is my grandfather, and he asked me to bring this to you. He said it was really important," she told the chief as he took the folder.

"Thank you, it's their report on the mur...." then stopped himself as he started to explain. It didn't matter. Phoebe was already in on the secret, but she was careful not to reveal it. Now she was an insider.

"I have to hurry back home."

He called out to her as she was going out the front door. "Tell him I'll be there in about half an hour."

Phoebe didn't drive directly back to Horace's house. Instead, she used the time to walk quickly down the street to the Western Union office. She knew the message pads were kept in a cubbyhole at the counter. She took one, wrote her uncle Theo's address and the message: "Epsilon. The game's afoot. Holmes Watson need you & Toby." At the conclusion of the message, she printed her name Phoebe Epsilon. The first and last words would get his attention.

Phoebe handed it to Norbert Hansen, the telegrapher who came out of retirement to work two of the slower afternoons a week. He told his coffee friends at the Green Parrot and his brother Odd Fellows at the lodge it was just to stay sharp. They nodded in agreement, knowing he needed the money. "You sure you don't want to send it yourself?" he asked. "Case it's personal or something."

"No, you go ahead and send it. And I want to pay for special delivery. It needs to get there just as soon as possible," Phoebe added, pulling out her change purse and handed him three one dollar bills.

"Must be pretty special. Holmes and Watson? Bet you want to tell me what it's all about, now doncha?" he asked.

Phoebe smiled sweetly and said, "Wish I could. Gotta run. Bye Norbert, I mean, Mr. Hansen," she told him, delighted that since they were co-workers it was acceptable to call an adult by his first name. "Leave my change in the top drawer, please." At the door she suddenly turned around. "No, Mr. Hansen, you keep the change as a tip." His eyebrows shot up in surprise and delight.

She hurried home, parked, and burst into her grandfather's house. "Grandfather! Chief Clarke just told me that Miss Stymington was murdered! Is that true?"

All three adults turned to look at her in alarm. "Sit down! Thunderation! That man *is* wet behind the ears. Now, listen to me young lady. He should not have told you that. It's true, but that news cannot get out. Not yet, at least! Is that clear? You are not to mention it again until your mother, Doctor Howell, or I give you permission! Not until after the chief makes it official. Thunderation!" Horace roared at her.

He was angry, but then realized it was not his granddaughter's fault. "I'm sorry, Phoebe, but he never should have said anything, much less that. I'm not angry at you, but at the chief. Look, he told you the truth, and the hard fact is that Miss Stymington was murdered. Now, I don't want you to say anything to anyone about it. The news will get out soon enough, but if you have any questions, you come and see Doctor Howell or me. No one else. Understand? Not even Fred right now."

"Yes, Grandfather," she said solemnly, fighting back the tears. It scared her when he got angry. Then she saw him wink at her again. His outburst had all been a bluff, smoke and mirrors. Phoebe had to hide her smile. She was sure that if her mother had not been present he would have discussed the case in detail with her.

"I think we'd better get hold of Theo and Clarice and find out when they're going to be here. We'll need their help," Horace said.

"But Grandfather, you can solve this all by yourself. Well, you and Doctor Howell can do it. And Fred is around, and I can help," Phoebe protested. "There's no reason for you to ask Uncle Theo and Aunt Clarice to come right away. They'll be here soon, anyway."

"I appreciate the compliment, but I think this is one where we need your Aunt Clarice to help us out," Horace replied.

"Your aunt Clarice has become friends with many of the older women here in Saugatuck," Harriet explained. "She has coffee with them, plays bridge and mahjong, and goes to some of their meetings. She's closer to some of them than the rest of us put together, wouldn't you agree Beatrix?"

"Yes, I quite agree," Beatrix said.

"Sort of like a mole or a spy?" Phoebe asked.

"Exactly," Horace said. "A spy."

Phoebe said nothing. She had another worry on her mind. She had already sent a telegram to her aunt and uncle, and eventually he Grandfather was sure to find out.

"All right, you two skedaddle out of here before the chief comes. Beatrix and I don't think having you here right now is a good idea. Plus, we're going to have a come-to-Jesus-meeting with him about not telling tales out of school. We'll see you two later." Horace got up to usher them out the door.

"I got your report, and say, I almost spilled the beans to your granddaughter, I guess," the chief said as he sat down in Horace's study.

"Yeah, well you did spill the beans because she figured it out. She's a bright woman, and figured it out. Thunderation, that was a blunder! I told her to keep quiet about it, and she'll mind what I said, but I've got to tell you, that was a real blunder to make. Talking too much will ruin your career if you're not careful. Now, what do you think about the report?"

"Well, it pretty much covered everything you told me at the hospital, so it's consistent. And I guess it's up to me to declare it a murder and start the investigation," the chief said quietly.

"Yes, it is. But there are several things to consider before you do so," Beatrix said carefully.

"Such as?" the chief asked.

"To start with, you probably need to look for her next of kin. I understand she was a spinster, but there must be someone left in her family. Perhaps siblings, nieces, nephews, cousins. They need to be told right away. There is also the matter of beginning to draw up a list of suspects. Suspects with a motive to kill her, the opportunity and the means to do it. People just don't go around using a syringe to kill someone with digitalis," Horace said.

Chief Clarke rubbed his chin. "Yeah, you're right about all of that," he said, "All that, it's going to take time."

Yes, yes it is. Of course, you might get lucky, too. Someone might walk into your office and confess, but I wouldn't hold my breath expecting it to happen. There's another thing: 1 know I told you that Doctor Howell is the top forensic pathologist in the country, but I've had time to think it over. I believe you should have the body sent to Lansing to have the state medical examiner do an autopsy. Or, to the state university medical school in Ann Arbor.

"There is one other thing, as well. You might find it beneficial to talk with Doctor Landis about Miss Stymington, specifically to investigate whether she has ever presented with any type of heart trouble," Beatrix added.

"Why?" the chief asked.

"To rule out pre-existing heart problems. You should do it because you are the police chief, and very likely you will be working with him far into the future," Beatrix said flatly. "And. he would know about any other serious ailments for which she was being treated."

"As for the labs in Ann Arbor, it's because you're new on the job, new to police work, and you don't want people thinking you're a blowhard who won't listen to anyone but himself. Or, jump to conclusions. You send the body off and people will understand you're doing your job as a true professional," Horace told him.

"But what about the cost? That's tax payers' money...."

This time Beatrix interrupted. "Yes, taxpayers' money that is being spent wisely. It is in their own best interest. And while the ME is examining the deceased, you can plan how you are going to handle the newspaper reporters."

"To say nothing about all the questions people here in town will be asking you," Horace added.

The chief's face dropped. "I hadn't thought of that. It's a lot easier writing tickets for parking too long or keeping kids and their bikes off the street."

"I agree. This way you can buy yourself a little time by sending the body to Lansing. Tell people that she is indeed dead, but you are waiting to hear back about the cause of death," Horace said.

"I guess you're right. And I can start finding some leads," the chief said. "I'd better get cracking. Are you two sure you want to play it this way? Won't it look like I don't have faith in you?"

"We've experienced that before. No, it won't damage our egos. Remember, we're the ones suggesting it. Sometimes, having extra time can be a very good thing. It makes a murderer jumpy," Horace said.

"Yeah?" the chief asked.

"A jumpy murderer often reveals their hand," Horace told him.

FIVE

"Now what?" Horace asked Beatrix after he had seen Chief Clarke out the door.

"I assume you meant what are we going to do next to solve the murder?" Beatrix asked, as she blew out the match she has used to light a cigar.

Horace smiled. "Yes. We know we've been conscripted. What do we do next?"

"Somehow," Beatrix said slowly, "somehow, I think we have to make some inroads into the women's social life in Saugatuck. That will not be easy."

"Well, you're a woman. Can't you do it?" Horace asked. "Just until we send for Theo and Clarice, and they get here."

"Congratulations on your observation of my gender, but spoken like a man. No, it is not that simple."

"Why ever not?" he asked in surprise.

"Horace, once people learn that Miss Stymington is dead, her friends and associates will circle the proverbial wagons. Especially her women friends. I am not one of them. Individually, or even as a group, they may have detested her or even hated her, but the situation has now changed and so will their behavior. She will receive instant sainthood and will be worshipped with accolades by her devotees. Not in the ecclesiastical sense of the word, of course, but there will be nothing but praise for her. No one will have anything unpleasant to say, and they will attack anyone who attempts to tarnish her newly minted sterling reputation."

Horace looked at her and said nothing, taking it all in, turning it over in his mind. All he could say was a bland, "I see. Sounds to me like it's a different set of rules."

"It *is* a different set of rules," Beatrix said firmly. "Always remember that the rules keep changing, alliances shift, and it is not logically established. Meanwhile, newcomers are not wanted or welcomed until they prove themselves."

"Sort of makes me yearn for the good old days of Al Capone and Frank Nitti," Horace growled.

"We did tell the chief that we would help him," Beatrix reminded him.

"Maybe we'll get lucky and someone will walk into his office and say he did it. Or she, as the case may be. That would be the end of it right then and there," Horace said.

"Oh, Horace, that would not be any fun," Beatrix pretended to pout. Then, she suddenly became more serious. "It is a bit morbid that we enjoy this, do you not agree?"

"Not really. The mortality rate remains at one hundred per cent, and all we are doing is investigating the ones who were murdered. We're not doing the murders," he answered wearily. Her obsession with the topic was tiresome. "It keeps the brain stimulated."

"We could always do cross-word puzzles," she suggested.

"What in the world is a crossword puzzle?" Horace asked.

"It's a sometimes challenging word game in the newspapers where clues are given for words of a specific length on the grid, either vertical or horizontal.They can be very diverting, and the more challenging ones are stimulating for the brain. It has been popular for over a decade. It surprises me that you are not aware of them."

"Well, I've been busy. I take it that you have done this?" Horace asked.

She smiled. "Yes, for the past year," Beatrix answered.

"I didn't know that."

"You do not know all my secrets," she smiled. "This diversion from Miss Stymington is getting us nowhere. I believe you are right to suggest we need Clarice. Meanwhile, there is also Fred."

"There is indeed Fred. Good thought." Horace pushed a button on the underside of his desk to call him. If he was in his apartment he would hear it and soon be down and in the office. He gave him a minute, then pushed the button a second time. "Must be out," Horace growled.

To their surprise, he came in through the front door, rushing through the house, and stopping just long enough to knock on the study door. "Thought you would want to know that that there Miss Stymington from the fancy poesy sniffing tea sipping society died this morning. It wasn't expected, so I thought maybe you'd know if the story is true," he blurted out.

"What story might that be, Fred?" Beatrix asked coolly.

"That she was flat out murdered. And in a church, no less! Bashed across the side of the head with a skillet. Any rumor to that truth, Boss?" Fred asked.

"I believe there is considerable truth to that rumor," Horace said cautiously. He wanted to encourage Fred to tell them what he had heard. "But never mind. Yes, she was found dead this morning."

"More to it than that?" Fred asked.

"The police chief has not yet released the details, but yes. It is a very suspicious death. And keep that to yourself, please," Beatrix said.

"Let me guess, you two got yourselves in on solving it, and you're about to tell me you'd like me to go have coffee, maybe get my shoes polished and hair cut, scout around a little and see what I can find out. Right?"

"That's about the size of it, Sergeant. We need someone to scout around a bit. And, isn't this the night the Odd Fellows hold their monthly meeting? The members might have some information," Horace asked. "So, yes, we need you."

"Yes, Sir, You're right about that! They're meeting tonight! Should be a big turn-out on account of the fact that they take next month off for a summer vacation. Say! That means there'll be a big feed, too, on account of it. Guess I'd better shave and put on a fresh collar and go there to see what I can hear," he said excitedly.

"That would be helpful," Horace said.

Fred was elated. He stood at attention, saluted Doctor Horace, and did a precise military style about-face to leave the room.

"Before you go out on your scouting mission, Sergeant ," Beatrix said cautiously. "Please remember that people will know she is dead, but not the cause of death. That must remain a military top secret. Not a word."

"Yes, Sir! Got it, loud and clear. I mean, yes, ma'am!"

"What do we need to do next?" Horace asked.

"You may not have noticed that it is now nearly five o'clock and all we have had is coffee today. I believe food is in order. Please do not offer to 'rustle up something' as Fred says. Phoebe has told me about your culinary talents," Beatrix said.

"There's always your place," Horace suggested.

Beatrix worked hard to stifle a chortle. "I do not cook," she told him.

"C'mon, you can't be serious," he answered.

"I am quite serious. For years I have always taken my meals at the hospital cafeterias. I continue to do so. I believe God created coffee shops, diners, and restaurants so that women could be spared the drudgery of the kitchen," she smiled.

"Oh," Horace said, perplexed.

"Besides, it is impossible for me to cook. I do not own neither pot nor pan," she told him.

"Really?" he asked.

"Really," she answered. "My suggestion is dinner in town."

Horace was still stunned at the news. "What say we walk over to the Butler for a light supper?"

"That is a very good suggestion A change of scenery will do us good, and Socrates always believed that walking was the best way to think. Shall we go?" Beatrix asked. "By the way, Horace, it is none of my business, but who cleans your house, makes your bed every morning, cooks, and does your laundry? I know Mrs. Garwood used to do it on the *Aurora,* but you have a house in town now."

Horace coughed, reached for his pipe and pouch, and stalled for time. "Well, Mrs. G found someone to, ah, come in and manage things."

"Yes, still living in a comfortable cocoon," Beatrix said flatly.

They had almost stepped onto the porch when the telephone in Horace's study rang, and he turned and hurried to answer it. Bobbie's voice came on the line. "Doctor Balfour, you have a *long distance telephone call!*" she said with urgency. "I believe it is from your sister-in-law in Minnesota. Please wait while I make the connection.'"

"Horace, dear, it's Clarice. A little birdie hopped upon my window sill, cocked a shining eye and said, 'you've got someone dead.'"

"Let me take one guess that this little birdie wasn't a canary. A Phoebe, perhaps?" he chuckled.

"Yes, the one and only. We received a very discreetly written telegram about Holmes and Watson and what must be their new adventure. It was addressed to Theo. I hope it was Phoebe being cryptic and not referring to Theo and me as bloodhounds," Clarice told him. "You still have Fred to sniff around, I trust."

"We could use you down here right now. Now look, Clarice, this isn't a private line so I won't say much. But we'd be grateful if you'd throw some glad rags into a Chesterton and hop a train down here. Both of you."

"Understood. Theo should be back from fishing in a little while. I'll tell him and we'll pack tonight. If we take the milk train to Brainerd first thing in the morning we can get to St Paul by noon and be on the Empire Builder into Chicago by this time tomorrow, and then come up on the train to.... oh, whenever it goes."

"It'll be late, so plan on staying here, would you?" Horace asked.

"All right, but I don't want you to fuss. And for pity's sake, don't try your hand at cooking anything!" Clarice teased. "Bye for now. Hold the line a second. Horace, glad rags, Chesterton, and hop a train? Just what century are you living in?"

"Clarice," Horace told Beatrix after he put the earpiece back the cradle. "Re-enforcements are moving up to the front. Good news. And the second comment about my cooking in less than ten minutes."

"Indeed. And then?" Beatrix asked.

"There's the question; what do we do next? I don't know. I'm open to ideas." Horace said as they started walking down the street.

"As we are going out, I would suggest a stop at the pharmacy so you can buy some cigars for me. I seem to have gone through several this afternoon," she told him. "I will, of course, insist on reimbursing you."

"Drug store? Say, that gives me an idea. How about a light meal and....?"

She cut him off. "Do not add a Green River phosphate to that idea." She changed her focus when she noticed Reverend Dederson from the Episcopal Church walking up the hill. "There is a starting point," she said. "He might have information or a clue."

Horace winced, hoping to avoid the cleric because he was certain he would say something about not seeming him in church. He was right.

"You seem to be a very busy chap," Dederson said as he shook hands with Horace. "We miss seeing you at divine services. Not a good example to set for your granddaughter, you know. Or, your daughter-in-law, for that matter."

"Nothing personal, padre. Between moving into a new house and my partnership with Doctor Landis...," Horace said quietly.

"Sometime, we should have a word about doctrine," Reverend Dederson interrupted him. "Phoebe told the confirmation class that you have an interesting perspective. I would like to hear more. She made it seem quite scandalous."

"Yes, well....." he sputtered.

"Good. Say, tomorrow morning? I'll come over to your office around nine or so. Perhaps your secretary can work me in between patients. You cure the body; I am the curate for the soul. We should aspire to being evenly yoked together. Good evening, doctors," he told them, touching the brim of his hat as he continued on his way.

"You'll have *such fun* tomorrow," Beatrix teased.

He answered with a throaty growl, "Thunderation."

Fred saw Dr. Horace's lights on in his study when he came back from the lodge meeting, and knocked on the door. He reached a hand up to loosen the knot on his tie, then thought better of it. The boss always wore a tie, even in his own home, and Fred thought he ought to wait until later to remove it.

"Any news from the front?" Horace asked.

"Some, but it all comes out the same. Everyone heard that that Miss Stymington died, and not one of the brothers seemed any too much cut up by it. It sort of reminds me of the new second lieutenant who got himself killed. You remember the one I mean, always chewing someone out, making demands, trying to makes sure everyone knew he was an officer. A whizz-bang got him. Not a scratch on him, but the concussion done did the job. And no one minded. Not one bit. Well, same thing with that there Miss Stymington. Sorry it happened, but no one's crying up a storm over it."

"I get the general idea. But Fred, anything beyond that?" Horace asked. "That's what we need – suspects and motives."

"Not a lot. A couple of the brothers, they're married and their wives had dealings with her. Not pleasant ones, either, and they both said that the dead lady made life miserable for their missus. Always wanting them to do something, then telling them it wasn't done the right way. One time I guess she was in charge of some big *do* at the literary club, and she told a woman, right then and there in front of everyone, that she had no taste in clothes or food. That sent her home in tears, and I guess the two of them never got on.

"Pretty much stuff like that. Same thing, just different times, dates, and names. Guess she must have been a tough one to be around. She's not like Mrs. Walters, or Doc Theo's wife, and if you don't mind me saying so without thinking that I'm butting in, and not like Doctor Howell, either. Goes to show you why that Miss Stymington never married, if you ask me."

"All right, Fred. It's getting late. Say, speaking of Clarice. She called this evening just after you went out. She and my brother are coming in by train tomorrow night or the next day. Thought you might like to know," Horace told him.

Fred smiled. "That sure is good to hear. And say, you know who joined up with the Odd Fellows? Captain. Captain Gar! I saw him there tonight. And say, there's another thing. I got to thinking that if we got a murder on our hands, maybe we ought to move that little signal cannon up here and put on your front lawn. Now, that way...."

Horace held up his right hand to stop the conversation. "Fred, the last thing we need is a cannon here as a lawn ornament."

"Well, I know that and you know that, and probably Captain Gar's got that figured out, too. But the way I look at it, if people are staring at that there cannon they won't have much time to look at a mighty fine crop of weeds you got growing. Besides, Mrs. G, she sort of wants to get rid of it, you see. I was sort of kinda thinking that we could help him out a little, and then that there cannon would be handy if we needed it."

"I'm sure she does. Tell you what, tomorrow you stop off at the Village Hall and see if they've got a use for it. Maybe put it in a park or something so they can shoot it off on Decoration Day and the Fourth of July," Horace told him.

"And don't forget Armistice Day. The boys could load it up and shoot it off. Blanks, of course. Make a real nice tribute to the war dead."

"Tomorrow, you see if you can make that happen. It's late and I'm going to bed." Horace was pleased with himself. He'd just given Fred an assignment that would keep him busy for a few hours.

SIX

"Good of you to see me, Doctor Balfour," Reverend Dederson said as he sailed into Horace's office at the hospital. "I haven't seen much of you at church lately. Is everything all right?" He sat down in an arm chair, flashing what Horace had sometimes thought of as a "padre's smile of deepest insincerity."

"Well, as I said last evening, between getting settled into a new home and a new practice, I've been a tad busy."

"That is understandable. But just as you care for your home and your work, I believe it is important for a man, especially in these hectic times, to remember to care for his soul," he said encouragingly to the point of sounding patronizing.

"Yes, I am sure you are right."

"But from what your granddaughter said several weeks ago, perhaps you are troubled by what you see as a certain rigidity in the church because of its doctrine. Am I correct?"

"Yes. I think it is important for everyone to think for themselves and ask questions," Horace said firmly, looking directly into Reverend Dederson. He was not yielding ground, adding, "On all subjects. All."

"Even in times of moral dissipation and a quest for material wealth? Don't you think that having structure is important to counter it?" The cleric's smile remained steadily in place.

"Not always. If surgeons always followed medical doctrine there would be no advances. Same thing for engineers, authors and artists, and more. Maybe for the church, too. I think Reverend Dederson, we disagree. And while I have you here, I need your help on something else; Miss Stymington."

"Yes, I know the news," he said mournfully, instantly adopting a funereal tone of voice, the smile slithering from his face. "I understand she had once been a member of my church but had a difference of opinion with a predecessor which is perchance the reason she chose to leave."

"I see," Horace answered, frustrated that he wasn't going to get additional information.

"It is uncharitable to speak ill of the departed, but I understand some of the women in the auxiliary at the time also found her, shall we say, challenging?" The cleric maintained his sad demeanor.

"Well, thank you for stopping by. It appears that we will have to agree to disagree and doctrine. Your information about the late Miss Stymington reconfirms what I have already heard," Horace said, standing up from his chair and walking towards the door. "Thank you. Perhaps we will talk again."

"Same song, same chorus. Thunderation!" Horace growled to himself when he was alone in the room again.

Fred was waiting for a chance to see Dr. Horace, and knocked on the door frame just as soon as the cleric was gone. "Boss, thought I ought to come by to let you know we got a wire from Doc Theo that him and the missus are at the station at St Paul waiting for the Empire Builder train. It's right on time. Here's the telegram for you," Fred said, handing Horace the thin paper.

"That's the best news of the morning. Thank you, Fred. I don't suppose I could trouble you to go over to their cottage and open it up for them? It's probably a bit musty after being closed up so long."

Fred smiled. "I'm one step ahead of you, Boss. I already done did that, and I made sure there was some coffee in the pantry, and I called the fellow who delivers the ice, and they're going to have a fresh block in the ice box, so things should be good and cool in there. I figured I'd pick up some milk and the mixings for flapjacks, butter, things like that later on today. Anything else? Oh, and some eggs and bacon, maybe a loaf of a bread. Maybe I ought to pick up a ring of bologna, too."

"Yes. Yes there is. Let's go down to the police station. I want to see Chief Clarke."

"I wouldn't do that if I was you on account of the fact that you'd miss him."

"Any idea where he went?"

"Yes, sure thing. He's out in the antercom right now, waiting to see you!" Fred chuckled. "Guess I got you on that one, didn't I?"

"Yes. Now show him in. And maybe you ought to be in on this conversation."

"Chief, I don't know if you've met Fred. Officially, he's my driver, right hand man, but he does a lot more than that. I'd be lost without him. Now, I've known him since I served with him on the Western Front. He's the soul of discretion, so I think he should be in on everything," Horace said. "And for what it's worth, he knows an assortment of very interesting characters who prefer not to talk with John Law."

"Your orderly, I take it," the chief said.

"A lot more than that. In a way; in a way he's my boss. You see, I was just a lowly one star brigadier, but Fred earned his stripes coming up through the ranks. What you might not know is that it was the sergeants who ran the army, not the general officers. So, tell me what you know, if you don't mind going first?"

"Not much, other than that folks put on a good front about that Miss Stymington, about how active she was in Saugatuck. Shoulder to shoulder tight; circle the wagons tight. Quite the society dame, as my mother would say of a woman like that. But then you press them a little and..."

Horace interrupted, "and it's quite a different story. Fred and I have heard the same thing time and again. And this is a case where it's what isn't said that is as important as what they do say."

"Meanwhile, I got the editor of the Commercial Record hot on my trail wanting to know what's going on, and another one from the Holland paper. You got some advice for me?" Chief Clarke asked.

"Yes. Tell them the truth. It's straight gospel truth that she died and that Doctor Howell and I did an autopsy, and now you are asking the doctors at the big hospital in Ann Arbor to give a second opinion. Tell them we agreed to it, if you like. Tell them you wanted to do it, if that will help. Until then, there isn't much else you can say. Meanwhile, you've got other work to do such as finding the next of kin."

"No one seems to know anything. That's the problem."

"All right, that might not be a problem. I think we can help. Now if you get a judge to sign a warrant to search her house, and under the circumstances even a justice of the peace will be willing to do it, then find where she keeps her papers and pictures. Something will turn up," Horace told him. "The other idea is that you talk with Bobbie over at the switchboard. She's full of information."

"Boss, if you haven't got anything more useful for me to do than to help the chief here, then I'd be happy to do that," Fred offered.

"There you go, Chief. Get yourself a warrant and go searching. The way I understand it, if you need to take some of the papers back to the office it's legal because it is part of your investigation. If you find out she's got relatives, then you'll probably want to give them a call and get them over here."

"That sounds like a good plan," the chief said with a big smile. "Fred, you ready to go investigating?" He was about to leave and asked, "I don't suppose you know how discreet Bobbie is down to the telephone?"

"You can count on her to keep quiet. If you ever want to be extra safe with a message, go down to Western Union and have my grand-daughter do it. She works there," Horace said.

"Not much I like better than to help out, Captain," Fred inter-rupted. "Say, you think we ought to see if Doctor Howell wants to tag along?"

Before the chief could answer, Horace said, "Good idea. You might find her in the lab. But listen you two, my guess is you'll be tagging along with her. Fred, you already know her methods. Chief, I know you're running the show, but you might be better off if you give her a free rein."

"Why's that?" the chief asked.

"A couple of reasons. First, she'll use her skills as a pathologist, and second, she's a woman, and she'll have a better idea where another woman would keep her secret stash of papers."

"Between you and me, Doc Howell has her own ways, all right," Fred added.

Doctor Balfour said, "Fred's right. She has her own ways. She's got a brilliant mind, and where she excels is making connections. When you get to Miss Stymington's house I can tell you right now, she'll tell you to be quiet and let her go into a room first. She'll stare at everything and it is like she's making a moving picture in her mind. She sees everything. Later on, she'll start making connections."

"Pardon me for saying so, Doc, but you're confusing me," the chief said.

"Don't apologize. It's the best I know how to explain her. You'll see for yourself. Just trust her. Like the boss said, just give her a free rein."

The trio tried the front and back doors of Miss Stymington's house and found them both locked. "Window?" Chief Clarke asked.

"That's a lot of work climbing through a window. Now, this isn't exactly legal-like, Chief, so if it makes you feel a little better, maybe you'd like to turn your back while I try something," Fred suggested.

The chief turned around and waited far less than a minute before Fred said, "Sure enough, I guess that there door really *was* unlocked the whole time. Just took a little encouragement." He folded up a packet of dental tools and put them back in his pocket. "Ladies first, Doc," he said, holding the door open for Doctor Howell.

"Please wait outside for a few moments while I look at everything and think," Beatrix said. "It will be best if I am not distracted." Fred gave the chief a knowing look and held a finger up to his lips. They stood still, letting her focus on the entrance hall, the parlor to the left, and the dining room to the right. "From the outside we know that there is at least another room plus the kitchen in the back. We will start there. Very carefully open up the kitchen drawers and let us see what we can find." Beatrix moved on to the other downstairs room. The door was locked.

"Fred, this door seems to be stuck. Would you come here, please?"

"Seems a bit odd," he said. "Most folks are content with a skeleton key on the inside doors, but she's had it switched out for a Yale." He chuckled, adding, "at least this here unit is pretty straight forward." For the second time he applied the metal probe and then the rake, then with a twist heard a satisfying snap. "All yours, Doc."

Beatrix stood in the doorway, quickly surveying the room. "Gentlemen, if you please, this is the room we should search first."

The chief carefully opened the closet door to look at the contents. On the shelves were several ledgers and boxes, and there were more boxes on the floor. "Looks like old calendars, diaries, and a lot of correspondence," the chief said, then sneezed. "And a lot of dust, too."

"Yes, dust. None of these things have been touched for a very long time," Beatrix said.

Beatrix went to the desk, then motioned for Fred. "Once more, if you please," she asked, pointing to the lock on a desk drawer.

"Doc, with this type of lock you could have opened it yourself with one of those there bobby-pins," Fred said. He smiled and added, "Glad to be of service, if you want to know the truth."

She carefully slid the drawer open, looked at the contents and quietly said, "Gentlemen, I believe we have found everything we need. Address book, her calendar for this year, letters, notes. Did you find anything in the cupboard, Chief?"

"Old ledgers, correspondence, and things like that? They might be helpful," he answered.

"Indeed. I would suggest you take all of it down to the station house to review it, Chief," Beatrix proposed.

"Well, you see, the thing is, Doctor, I don't know when I'll get a chance to read all of it. Much of it, to be honest. You don't think you'd have time, by any chance, do you? And, I don't think we ought to leave it here in case someone wants to..."

"Yes, you are quite right. We are fortunate so far no one has purloined the letters, to misquote Edgar Alan Poe. They must be secured." Beatrix turned to Fred and asked, "Fred, do you think Doctor Horace would object ...?"

"He won't scream bloody murder if we brought anything into his house to solve this here crime, if that's what you mean. The fact of the matter is there's a closet just inside the front parlor and I know for a fact he's never once opened the door. I don't know if he even knows it's there. I think all this evidence would be safe there."

"Then, gentlemen, I suggest we finish searching this room, do the same upstairs, and take the evidence with us when we leave," Beatrix said with tremendous satisfaction.

"I don't want to question your line of thinking," the chief said slowly, "but if we found everything we need, then I can't see the point."

"We need to be thorough, and we might not have this opportunity again. Let us proceed," Beatrix said.

SEVEN

"I was surprised to learn that you and Doctor Theo did not spend the night at Horace's home," Beatrix said to Clarice late the next morning when the two women met outside the Colonial Hotel for coffee. Clarice moved toward her to give Beatrix a hug and kiss on the cheek, then paused, remembering how the gesture made her uncomfortable, and held open the door.

"That was my doing, I'm proud to say. I know it disappointed Horace, and I'm sure he spared no effort, but if we had taken him up on his offer, Theo and Horace would have sat up half the night, and we'd already had a long day. He offered, but I put my foot down. All of us needed our rest, especially Theo. Now, enough of that. Tell me about this murder," Clarice said, her eyes widening with excitement.

Beatrix leaned closer to Harriet, took a breath and said, "Well....." and for the next fourteen minutes told her everything she knew.

"So, someone finally did in Miss Stymington? I'm half-surprised it didn't happen ages ago."

"That is a bit strong, is it not?" Beatrix asked, surprised at how casual Clarice seemed to sound.

"Perhaps. She was a very intelligent and capable woman, but she had the ability to hurt people with just a look or the tone of her voice. She could be mean to others just for the sake of being mean. I think she reveled in it. Last summer there was a reception at the little red chapel over near Shorewood. One of the women had rented it for her daughter's graduation party. Miss Stymington came in, draped her handbag over the back of a chair and said to another woman who wanted to sit at the same table. "No, you can't sit here. It's just for my friends and me."

"That was dreadful," Beatrix gasped.

"Yes, but that was typical of her. It is typical of a number of the women. They never missed an opportunity to hurt someone's feelings. So, as I said, I'm half-surprised she wasn't murdered years ago. Tell me, was it a knife in the back? That wouldn't surprise me. She was always doing it to others. Poetic justice if it was, if you ask me."

"No, but if you care to help me go through some of the papers Chief Clarke took from her home, we might have a better idea for a motive and suspect," Beatrix suggested.

"Paperwork it is!" she said brightly. "It will give me something useful to do. Knowing Theo, he will probably stay at the hospital until Horace is ready to come home, unless he goes off roaming with Fred somewhere. I know he'll want to see Captain Garwood, and then that will lead to renting a boat and fishing." When they returned to Horace's house Beatrix showed her the closet full of boxes. Clarice gasped, "Oh, my! There is a lot of paper. Where do we start and what are we looking for?"

"The good news is that Chief Clarke took the rest of the papers – three boxes of them – to the police station."

"Three more? Why?"

"He took the most recent papers to look for next of kin, finances, and who knows what all else. I believe he has insufficient experience to do a thorough job," Beatrix explained. "There is an apron in the kitchen. You might want to wear it. Dust."

"Any idea what we are hoping to find?" Clarice asked.

"That is the unknown question at the moment," Beatrix said carefully. "We do not know. We do not know what or who we are looking for, or even when. Perhaps a name that continually comes up, especially in a diary, an old bill or note of money she loaned someone, or borrowed from. It could be something out of the ordinary." She paused. "Or, it could be something very ordinary."

"That's not much to go on," Clarice said quietly.

"No, but Miss Stymington was killed by poison, and poison is usually a woman's first weapon of choice, not a gun or knife." Beatrix paused and gently giggled, "Not even a knife in the back! To our knowledge she never married or had children, so that might rule out an angry husband or aggrieved children. Then again, it might have been a niece, nephew, or cousin waiting for their rich aunt to die and leave them a fortune. Perhaps they were in a hurry and become impatient."

"I always thought it was a rich uncle," Clarice sighed. "What if we use the triage method, one box at a time. We set aside anything that is obviously unhelpful, put possibilities in another pile, and then possible genuine clues in another. That way, if we need to, we can go through the second and third piles again later on."

"That appears to be a reasonable plan," Beatrix said. "Horace works best with a pipe; I prefer a cigar. Would it bother you?"

"No, not at all," Clarice laughed. She paused for a moment, then hesitatingly asked, "Truth be told, I've always wanted to try one, but never dared. Would I be absolutely shameless if I dared ask to borrow one?"

"No, that would not be shameless. But I will give you a cigar so you do not need to give it back if it is not to your liking," Beatrix told her. The two women slowly made their way through all of the papers and documents, whittling it down to two piles of potentially helpful information – finances and her old desktop diaries. The rest of it was unhelpful at best, and soon put back into the boxes. "I truly hate to say this, but I think you are far better at finding connections in her personal finances," Clarice yawned.

"Yes, I believe you are correct and will do it later," Beatrix answered. "Shall we look at her calendar?" The two women sat side by side at the table, making their way through several years of appointments, meetings, and social events.

Suddenly, Beatrix stood up. "I must go for a walk." Without any explanation she walked out of Horace's house, leaving Clarice wondering what might be wrong. She quickly remembered that Beatrix would abruptly walk off if she needed to think.

She returned less than an hour later, and without explaining her sudden absence, began talking. "Her hand-writing is consistent over the years, and that is highly unusual for anyone, but especially for someone her age. She uses initials. Notice how every five weeks, the same time and the same day, she wrote, 'HD'. At first I thought it might stand for the initials of an individual. But then I remembered in the morgue noticing that she dyed her hair. I believe she had a treatment about seven to ten days ago but the chief has her recent diary. We do not need it. HD could mean hair dresser or hair dye, the choice of which is immaterial. If we look at her calendar about every five weeks we should see an appointment and time jotted down." The two women flipped the pages, and Beatrix was pleased her deduction was correct. "That would not be something she would want another woman to know, thus the initials."

"Well done, Sherlock!" Clarice told her. "How *very interesting!* I wonder if the other girls know?"

"Elementary," Beatrix teased in return. "Have you discovered anything more?"

"Well, I think that is fascinating information, don't you? We know she has her hair touched up!" Clarice said.

"May we focus on the murder and not salacious gossip?" Beatrix asked.

"I think so. She went to countless committee meetings for every organization in town – charities, improvement groups, arts, literature and the flower and tea group. All of them in the calendar. But then, at the end of it, single letters, initials, and behind each of them a number from one to five. For example, an 'R' which I think means refreshments, and whether it met with her approval or not, on a scale of one to five. As for the initials, MB – Muriel Bensen, PV for Penelope Vandenberg, and so on. I think I know most of them, or can figure them out, and I assume the numbers are whether or not they lived up to her standards, on a scale of one to five."

"How positively wicked! There is so much pain in the world, Beatrix exclaimed in dismay. "I hate to ask this, but are your initials in her diary?"

"Oh yes," Clarice said with disgust. "CB, and never more than a two. That miserable little cow!"

"I am afraid that is what readers of another's diary often discover. I am truly sorry, Clarice," Beatrix said softly. "I should not have asked you to help."

"So help me, after reading her critique, if someone hadn't done her in first I would have asked her in front of everyone else who dyes her hair because they do such a wonderful job making it look so natural!" Clarice fumed.

Beatrix's eyes widened. "Clarice! That is the answer! Someone, someone she thought was a friend, or who once thought of her as a friend, got to her ahead of you. I suspect you were exaggerating when you just said that you would publically humiliate her, but she has constantly belittled and humiliated others. And at least one of them had the motive and opportunity to murder her. As I said, poison is a woman's first choice of a weapon. Well done, Clarice!"

"Oh!" she said in surprise. "I had no idea. But which one of her alleged friends did it?"

"*Fiends* might be a better choice of words. That is the question. Meanwhile, we should put aside the financial ledgers and the diaries, and put the rest of the boxes back in the closet," Beatrix answered. "Do you mind going through her diary and writing down the names and the critique numbers she gave? It might give us an idea of a suspect."

"A lot of suspects," Clarice sighed.

When Horace walked through the front door of his house into the parlor he was surprised to see Beatrix. "I just stopped by your house but you weren't there," he told her.

"No. I am here," she said flatly.

"Yes, well, I have some good news for you. Chief Clarke just called and he said that medical examiner in Ann Arbor concluded you made the perfect diagnosis – digitalis administered with a small hypodermic needle through the ear drum. They did an exploratory and found more of it in the canal. Well done and extra points for you, Doctor Howell."

"That is what I expected to hear, although it is good news to know I was right. Has he made any progress finding a next of kin?" Beatrix asked.

"No, not yet. He said you had all of the papers from her house, and was hoping you had some good news for him."

Clarice and I did not find an address book among her things. Has he looked in her handbag? Perhaps she carried it with her."

"I don't believe he has opened it yet," Horace said. "He's still squeamish about opening a woman's handbag."

"Oh, for pity's sake, it's a murder investigation!" Clarice said.

"Some men are not comfortable snooping in a private place like a handbag," Horace said. "Me included."

"If he is so squeamish about it, ask him to bring it over here and I'll do it," Clarice said firmly. "Men! May I use your telephone to call the police station?"

"Did you learn anything?" Horace asked Beatrix, adroitly changing the subject when Clarice walked into his study.

"Yes. We are very convinced that Miss Stymington was killed by a woman. Almost everyone in her social circle would have had ample motive," Beatrix reported. "I believe it narrows the list down to about a dozen possible suspects among them alone. Perhaps there are others. Clarice and I may pare it down even more tomorrow."

"And how are you so certain?" Horace asked.

"One of Clarice's friends is holding a card party – bridge – tomorrow afternoon and I have been invited to join them. I am sure some of them will give us some indication."

"Don't you find it a bit odd that they're having a party just a couple of days after one of their friends died?" Horace asked.

"Yes, but we no longer live in the Victorian Era, either. No black wreath on the door. No black arm bands. No full morning for a year."

That evening, as they were walking before sunset Horace suddenly stopped and turned to Beatrix. "You said you are going to a card party tomorrow? I know you play whist, but bridge is different. Very different."

"Yes. I have played it. The last time was in 1913. It was July 26th, to be more accurate, I was one of several pathologists invited to see Dr. Plummer's laboratory in Rochester. He is a very gracious but quite odd genius, and his wife was absolutely insistent that I stay at their home rather than the Damon Hotel, so I accepted their invitation.

"That evening they decided to play cards with Doctor and Mrs. Sheard, but then Doctor Sheard was called to the hospital, so I was asked to sit in. I found bridge far more interesting than whist, more complex, and quite exhilarating. I felt quite giddy once I learned the system. When Clarice invited me to join her tomorrow I thought it might be diverting to play again, although I do not wish to make a habit of it. I must be careful not to yield to the temptation."

"Are you telling me you haven't played for almost a decade and a half and you're going to single-handedly take on a room full of women?" Horace asked.

"Oh, not single-handedly. Clarice will be there also, and she tells me that they will be having martinis. It is a drink, not the Martini-Henry 303 caliber rifle," Beatrix said. "They will undoubtedly enjoy themselves, but I will keep my wits by abstaining."

"Wise thinking," Horace said. "Glad to know you will be leaving the guns at home," Horace said, turning his head so Beatrix didn't see his smile.

"I believe that the other women will make considerable small-talk and gossip while playing bridge, and very likely become more animated and uninhibited by the second drink. Clarice said I should consider wearing a summer frock and advised me against having a cocktail. We want to keep a clear heads and perhaps find our killer. As Jordan Baker once said, 'It is a great advantage not to drink among hard-drinking people.'"

"Jordan Baker? Jordan Baker? Do I know him?" Horace asked.

"I doubt it. Jordan Baker is a fictional woman in Fitzgerald's *The Great Gatsby.*"

"I see," he said, "Beatrix, do you think a card game will be helpful?"

"I believe it might. We have gathered considerable factual information, and I do not it is moving the investigation forward. The gossip and small-talk may be far more revealing," she told him.

"I thought you despised small talk…..?" he asked.

"I do. I will be listening, not contributing."

MURDER OF THE SAUGATUCK CHURCH BASEMENT KITCHEN LADIES

EIGHT

Horace had agreed to meet with Chief Clarke at eight the next morning. "I went through her handbag, but I sure felt funny about doing it, and like you said, I found her address book," the chief said. "I gotta tell you, that wasn't an easy thing to do. Growing up, my ma would have used a belt on my behind if I'd so much as peaked in her purse, even if she'd left it open on the dining room table. Pa would have told me to go out and cut my own switch. And there I was yesterday, emptying a strange lady's possessions all over my desk."

"You'll never know what comes next in police work or surgery. And what did you find?" Horace asked.

"She has a sister living in Albany, New York, so I called her to let her know that her sister had passed away."

"That wasn't an easy call to make," Horace said gently. He shuddered slightly, remembering far too many times walking into a waiting room to give the family or friends the bad news.

"No, and she took it pretty rough at first. Then, she pulled herself together and said she'd come out here for the services and so on. She should be here in a couple of days. Funny thing is, she wanted to know if I found her bank savings book. Just like that. I figure maybe she's in a tight spot and needs some cash. Afterwards I called Archie over to the Commercial Record and told him I'd give him the news this morning. He should be here in a couple of minutes. I figured it would be best if you were here, too."

"Thank you, I think," Horace said hesitantly. The idea of talking with a news reported was never a safe and comfortable thing to do. "Remember to always conceal and never reveal."

The chief looked up. "Traveling man, are you?"

"Brother," Horace answered cryptically. It was a surprisingly comfortable thing to hear. They were both Masons, and he knew he could trust the chief.

They had barely enough time to lay out their plans before Archie Bessinger walked in a few minutes later. "Hiya Doc, Chief. I hear you got some news for me. Stymington woman, is it?"

"Yes," Chief Clarke said. "You already know of her passing, but we were not able to release the cause of death..."

"I hear tell she died of a heart attack," Archie interrupted. "That's what the boys over to the pool hall said. I just got the feeling there's more to the story, you two calling me in here and all."

"There is, so sit down and listen," the chief said. "Here's the deal, so hear me out. I'll give you the biggest scoop of your career, the sort of story that will get you hired by a big city paper, but you're going to do it my way or not at all. Got it?" "Sure," he said quickly, instantly seeing a brighter future.

"Your paper comes out this evening, doesn't it? And you and your editor want to sell a lot of papers, so it's in your best interests to keep your traps shut for a few hours. I'll give you the story, and you write it the way I give it, but mum's the word until two o'clock this afternoon," the chief said. "That means no talking to anyone and no early edition of the paper, you got it?"

"Sounds big. What gives?" Archie demanded. "But you can't stop the freedom of the press, you know!"

"I'm not, except you've gotta do it my way, or there's no story and you can go back and tell your editor he doesn't have a lead story after all. You get your story in return for helping with the investigation, and then you might have another big story thrown on your lap. Here's the way it's going to be: Like I said, you stay quiet until two, see. That's when you call the Vandenberg house, tell them how she died, and ask for any comments. Two o'clock, and not a minute earlier. That jake with you?"

"Sure," he said, confused.

"You double-cross me and I'll have you in a nice cold cell for interfering with police business. You understand?"

"Sure. Keep my trap shut until two and make a call. You got my word. Now, how did she die? Heart attack or something else?"

"She died of a heart attack, but it was caused by digitalis."

"What's that?"

"It's the foxglove plant," Horace started to explain.

"You mean she got killed by some flowers. My mother, now she sneezes around lilacs and marigolds, but I never heard of someone dying from flowers," Archie objected. "You pulling my leg? C'mon, be straight with me, wouldya?"

"There are a number of poisonous plants. A lot of them. Most of them are quite common, and people have them in their gardens," Horace explained. "Foxglove is one of them. In Latin it is digitalis – a type of poison."

"You don't say! Say, I gotta tell the boss about that one. He could use the power of the press to make them against the law!"

"Archie, can we just stick with Miss Stymington's murder, please?" the chief asked.

"Yeah, sure! But say, how'd they do it? Give her a nice bunch of them flowers, put the leaves in her salad, or something else?"

"Something else," Horace said. "They took the sap from the plant and injected it through her ear drum."

"Yeah, sure. Go ahead, pull the other one," Archie said, lifting up his foot. "Come on, stay straight with me, wouldya? I got a story to write and a deadline.'

"I'm giving it to you straight," Horace snapped.

"Archie, it's a murder case. I'm not releasing any more details until we apprehend the killer and the DA files the charges. Now, you have your story and you gave your word. I'll even throw in your headline: Saugatuck Socialite Murdered in Church Basement Kitchen," the chief said. He and Horace watched as the reporter wrote it down.

"Thanks, fellas. Gotta run!" Archie said, jumping up from his chair and making for the door.

"That went fairly well," the chief smiled.

"Yes, and within minutes everyone in town is going to know what happened. That's going to put everyone on their toes," Horace replied. "Meanwhile, I need to attend the living. Let me know if I can do anything to help."

"Say, there is one thing..." the chief began. "Find out who did this. Better, come back around two or so. I'd like to have this wrapped up by dinner. Tell you what, we wrap this thing up and I'll buy you a big Del Monaco steak, biggest they got, at any restaurant in town. You and Doctor Howell, both of you."

Horace laughed. "Better not, or Fred will have his nose out of joint being left out."

"Say, you're right. Him, too."

"The key to understanding these women is one word – competition. They compete with each other on everything. To make matters interesting, some of the women from town think they are the cream of society, but they don't know that the women who summer here from around Chicago laugh at them behind their backs. Meanwhile, the women from St Louis laugh at both the women from here and from Chicago because they are so pretentious," Clarice said as she and Beatrix walked to Mrs. Vandenberg's house.

"I do not understand it," Beatrix said. "It does not make sense."

"No. No it doesn't. They're competitive over everything – clothing, children, their husband's career, what they do in a club or church or anything else. That's why I encouraged you to wear your blue dress this afternoon. It's subtle, elegant, and may be a bit intimidating to a couple of the others."

"How very pathetic," Beatrix said barely above a whisper. "I am not certain I want to intimidate anyone."

"It all gets much worse. These women like to run things, but they don't roll up their sleeves and do the actual work. Most of them have an apron, but it's a fancy one for show and not for doing anything. And they constantly tell the other women members what to do and how to do it."

"Oh, my. I do not think I would want to be friends with them," Beatrix said.

"I agree with you. The important thing to remember this afternoon is that none of them are true friends, and be especially wary if any of them are too friendly."

"That also is pathetic," she answered.

"Yes, but there is nothing you and I can do about it. They are going to be absolutely ruthless for awhile because they are, well, Ruth-less."

"I do not understand," Beatrix said.

"It's a terrible pun, but just too irresistible. Now that Miss Stymington, *Ruth* Stymington, is dead the women will be jockeying for position to be the new queen bee, and therefore they are absolutely ruthless."

Beatrix giggled. "That is still a terrible pun. I think it is something Horace might say. I know some people think a pun is the lowest form of humor, but it is truly clever. It is good to know. I have my doubts one of them will slip up and reveal herself as the murderess."

"Well, here we go into the lion's den. Best foot forward and good hunting to both of us," Clarice said as they walked up the steps to the Vandenberg home.

The quest to take over from Miss Stymington had already begun. "Why don't I pour the coffee today?" Mrs. Benson offered.

"That is ever so kind of you, but don't you think I should do it since I have always poured tea at the opposite end of the table," April Grassle offered. "I believe it is traditional for tea to move up to coffee in her absence."

In the kitchen, Belva Leery was helping her hostess put some cookies on a silver tray, and saw an opportunity to take Mrs. Vandenberg down a peg. Just as soon as they put the trays on the table, Mrs. Leery said, loud enough for the whole room to hear, "I think you are so brave imitating some of the modern artists, dear."

"What do you mean?" Mrs. Vandenberg asked warily.

Pointing to a tray of cucumber open faced sandwiches, she said, "Well, most of us always are very careful to match the slices of bread with the ones next to it because it is symmetrical, more formal and traditional. But today, you are imitating some of the modernists with a-symmetrical crusts, as if you didn't have a care in the world? Isn't that amusing, girls?"

Mrs. Vanderberg did not look amused and tried to retake control of the room. She tapped a fork against a glass, and when she had everyone's attention, said, "Ladies, I am so grateful you could be here today even though it is such a sad occasion. We must pull together when we have lost one of our own, and then move forward. We have done it in the past, and I know, together, we can do it now. I know many of you always enjoy having a forbidden cocktail or two, or is it three for some of you, and you know who you are, but today is a somber one. We will restrict ourselves to white wine. Shall we lift our glasses and toast the memory of our dear, departed, Ruth Stymington. To Ruth!" The others echoed her toast. "Now, please enjoy the refreshments, even if some of you keep saying you are slimming, or trying to slim down." She looked across the room at the very matronly looking Millicent Gray.

A few of the women made a tentative move toward the buffet table, eager to sample the sweets, none of them daring to be the first because the others might think they were greedy. One of them finally picked up a small plate and cloth napkin. "The queen is dead," Clarice whispered to Beatrix. "Thus a new reign begins. Long live the queen."

Each of the women put one of each variety of tea sandwich on her plate, shuffled along, and took one each of the deserts. "Oh, bankett. Do try some, Beatrix. It's a Dutch dessert," Clarice urged.

"I am uncomfortable. It has the same aroma as...."

"Almonds. It is an almond pastry."

"I was thinking cyanide," Beatrix whispered in Clarice's ear. She thought it was in poor taste to serve it, considering the recent murder, and then realized only she and Clarice knew the cause of Miss Stymington's death.

A few moments later Mrs. Vandenberg once again rapped her fork against her wine glass. "Ladies, before we cut cards to partner up and begin to enjoy our bridge there are a couple of reminders. First, we will need a special committee to plan the reception for our dear Miss Stymington's funeral. And don't forget that two weeks from tomorrow we have our annual charity garden tour. We need to promote this and sell tickets, and of course we must remind the Almighty that it is his duty to provide perfect weather this year. We don't need a repeat of last year when it was a washout.

"Most importantly, of course, we must agree on a new president of our group, and that is something of very great urgency, considering the forthcoming garden tour. It must be someone worthy, someone with leadership skills and someone with impeccable taste. Perhaps one of you would care to nominate someone? Or perhaps yourself, if you believe that is appropriate…" she asked.

No one responded; each of them waiting for someone to go first, and all of them hoping they would be the nominee.

"Well, if no one is being nominated, I will proceed and nominate myself if that is acceptable to all of you," Mrs. Vandenberg said.

"She always wanted to be the head cheese," a woman standing just behind Clarice whispered to a nearby friend.

"Well-aged stinky cheese, too, despite all her trips to the beauty salon to touch up her grey roots," her companion whispered back.

Mrs. Vandenberg was quietly elected by general consensus.

Clarice and Beatrix moved toward a card table where Mrs. Gray was sitting. She turned and snapped at them. "You can't sit here. Those chairs are for my friends." Beatrix shuddered slightly. She had heard those same words, and in the same tone of voice, in high school and again in college. She's heard them again more recently at the reception after the ribbon cutting ceremony. Two women found a vacant table and were about to sit down when they were driven off by another. What she didn't realize was that Mrs. Gray was not angry at Beatrix and Clarice or even being territorial. She snapped at them because she was angry at Mrs. Vandenberg pushing herself forward – yet again. She had taken her frustration out on the two of them.

"So good to see you again Clarice," a woman said, then turned to Beatrix to introduce herself. "I am Mrs. Jennings and this is my life-long friend, Mrs. Franklin. Where are you from, Miss...?" she asked Beatrix.

"Howell. Beatrix Howell," she said quietly.

"I heard from one of the girls that you work in medicine. You must have been a doctor's secretary or a nurse?" Mrs. Jennings asked.

"No. I truly admire the work they do. However, I am a physician. More precisely, I have an advanced degree in forensic pathology. As of late, I have begun doing some private consulting work as a forensic artist." Clarice watched Mrs. Jenning's face drop. Beatrix had just put the woman in her place.

Beatrix was interrupted by Mrs. Franklin. "Oh, now I remember you! You and Clarice's brother-in-law also solve crimes! That is so very brave of you, my dear. You are so avant-garde, becoming a doctor, solving murders, and a consort to Dr. Balfour! There are so few truly modern women here!"

"I am hardly a consort or anything else with Doctor Balfour except as a medical colleague," Beatrix shot back at her, her eyes narrowed in rage.

Their conversations was interrupted by a telephone ringing in the kitchen. "Oh, my hired girl will take care of that. I told her I am not to be disturbed for anything other than a dire emergency," Mrs. Vandenberg said grandly to her table companions. A mantle clock had just struck two.

A few moments later the maid slightly opened the kitchen door and beckoned Mrs. Vanderberg to slip away from the table. The two whispered and Mrs. Vandenberg went into the kitchen. When she returned the color was gone from her face. She was ashen, and steadied herself against the side table.

"Ladies, my dear, dear sisters, truly, at a time like this. It is my unfortunate task to tell you that Miss Stymington's death did not come from natural causes. The police have announced it was pre-meditated murder." The women gasped in horror. "I understand we can read much more in detail this evening in that little weekly newspaper."

Mrs. Franklin leaned across the table toward Beatrix. "Did you know any of this?" she asked in a whisper.

"Yes. Doctor Balfour and I did the autopsy and I made the diagnosis. After that, I insisted that Chief Clarke order the body sent to Ann Arbor for a second opinion. Only he could announce that it was a homicide."

"How was it done?" Mrs. Franklin wanted to know.

"That is something I cannot divulge. I will simply say that all indicators make it clear that it was pre-meditated. Cold, calculated and meticulously planned."

Clarice leaned toward Mrs. Franklin, "Bunny, perhaps you have an idea who could be so cold and calculating as to do it."

Mrs. Franklin recoiled in disgust. Then she looked around Mrs. Vandenberg's living room, her eyes widening, then suddenly narrowing, and lips tightening. Could one of the other women be the murderer?

"With this horrible news now laid at our feet, I do not feel we could concentrate on the cards. Indeed, it would be inappropriate for us to do so. Since we have already concluded the business portion of this afternoon's gathering perhaps we should enjoy our refreshments and the comfort of one another before we say adieu. Please, please come back to the serving table for more."

The women stayed for another ten minutes or so, then began looking at the door. All of them were ready to leave, but none of them wanted to be the first. Those who remained were sure to engage in more cutting gossip, as always, about the first to leave. Clarice pressed her foot against Beatrix to get her attention, then barely nodded toward the buffet table. Millicent Grey was slowly working her way towards it, talking with her friends, until she stood in front of the treats. "And now we see the handkerchief in her right hand as she holds her plate," Clarice whispered. "One piece on the plate, several cucumber sandwiches on the handkerchief. Next dessert and repeat. Now she moves the plate to her left hand and slips the napkin into her already open handbag. Oh, I'm sure she is quite pleased with herself. She just got the last piece of blanket!"

"You are very wicked," Beatrix said to her.

"People watching is such fun, isn't it?"

Gradually, the women moved out of the dining room, into the foyer, and were ready to depart. Mrs. Vandenberg followed them out of the house to the doorstep, wishing them all a goodbye.

"Millicent, you look very flushed! Are you all right?"

Mrs. Grey turned toward her hostess, her face red and she was panting for air. "No. No, not..." and she collapsed onto the front lawn.

Girls, give her some room for some air!" Mrs. Franklin said.

"Should I call for a doctor?" Mrs Vandenberg asked. "Yes, yes, of course I must," she said, answering her own question. Instead, she stayed in place near the door, transfixed on the scene in front of her.

"I am a physician," Beatrix answered, hurrying to where Mrs. Grey collapsed.. "Clarice, I need you. With me, please. Now." The two women knelt in the grass on either side of Mrs. Grey. "Look for a carotid pulse," Beatrix instructed. Both women instinctively worked to help her, perhaps save her life.

"Call for the ambulance," Clarice ordered. "Mrs. Vandenberg, call an ambulance now!"

"There is no pulse," Beatrix said quietly. She watched Clarice's fingers tips search Mrs. Gray's right side of her neck, "No."

Before anyone could respond, Beatrix made a fist and gave Mrs. Gray a solid punch over the solar plexus. She looked at Clarice, who shook her head. "Again," Clarice said. Beatrix repeated the hit, but it did no good.

"What are you doing?" Belva Leery screamed at them. Clarice and Beatrix ignored her.

"They're trying to make her heart start up again," someone said to the women as they watched in horror, two or three of them openly crying, holding a hand over their mouth in shock.

Clarice swallowed hard and barely said, "Mrs. Vandenberg, would you bring a sheet or a tablecloth please. Mrs. Gray has passed away."

NINE

"Clarice, please listen carefully. Go back inside the house, and do not let anyone else come in. Lock the backdoor, please. I would like you to use a cloth, any clean cloth will do, when you turn the lock. Be careful when you do it. We do not want to smudge fingerprints. And, make sure nothing is touched inside the house. Will you do that, please?" Beatrix whispered to her.

"Yes, yes, of course," Clarice said breathlessly.

As she was going inside, Beatrix spoke loudly to the women standing on the front lawn. "Ladies, please, your attention. The ambulance will soon be here. I believe the police will also be attending, so all of us must stay here and not leave until Chief Clarke dismisses us." She looked at each woman, almost daring any of them to challenge her authority or debate the subject.

The ambulance arrived first, with Chief Clarke in his police car immediately following. To her relief, Horace got out of the passenger side of his car, carrying two black bags. His, of course, and also hers. Out of respect for authority, Horace followed behind the chief and handed Beatrix her bag. Immediately he knelt down besides Mrs. Gray and pulled his stethoscope from his bag, while Beatrix did the same. He listened for a heartbeat, moving it around her chest, then on her neck. With tightening lips, he shook his head and put the instrument back in his bag.

"Gone, just as you said. Are you all right?" Horace asked Beatrix when he was on his feet again. Then, more loudly than necessary, he told the chief, "Doc Howell was right. She was gone before we got in the vehicles." He turned to Beatrix and said, "Well done."

"Yes, and Horace, thank you for asking. The deceased is Millicent Gray. I do not know her age. She was at the party with the rest of us, and as we were leaving she stepped outside, collapsed, and died. It was instantaneous."

"Isn't Clarice here? I thought she was coming, too." Horace asked.

"Yes. The chief should know this, as well." They stepped closer to him. "I sent her inside to lock the back door and keep everyone out of the house. She is guarding it to make sure nothing is disturbed." Beatrix told him. "I hope that was an acceptable decision on my part."

"Are you thinking it is murder?" Chief Clarke asked.

"I have no way of knowing. However, the probability of murder is quite high, considering that she is the second member of this group to pass away suddenly and unexpectedly. I was sitting where I could see her face just after Mrs. Vandenberg came into the parlor to tell us that Miss Stymington had been murdered. Mrs. Gray looked very shaken."

"Heart attack?" Horace asked.

"That will be revealed. Horace, a very wicked thought crossed my mind. What if it was not murder....?" she whispered close to his ear.

Horace looked at her, his brow knotted. "A possibility she took her own life?"

"Or, she might have been over-come with shock that she had caused a murder," the chief said.

Before Beatrix could answer a somewhat battered, exhaust-spewing Model T delivery pick-up pulled in front of the house, and the driver tooted the horn. "I'll take care of it," Beatrix said. "It's Mickey Smith, Saugatuck's Flower Fairy."

"I have a delivery for Mrs. Vandenberg, but it doesn't look like this is a good time," the woman said.

"No, not at all. I do not know when would be a good time, other than this is not it. By the way, Miss Smith, who sent the flowers?"

"Oh, ah, ah Mrs. Gray. Millicent Gray."

"Thank you," Beatrix said quietly. "Miss Smith, when were the flowers scheduled to arrive?"

"Any time after two o'clock. Miss Gray always sends thank you flowers, and she said I could deliver them anytime after two and just go to the back door and put them on the kitchen counter. I guess she liked to surprise people that way." She snorted in derision. "I don't think anyone was ever surprised, really. She was predictable."

"Listen, Mrs. Vandenberg might find some comfort in them later on today. I'll just put them inside the front door," Mickey Smith said. "She'll be grateful since it's Mrs. Gray's last gift to her."

Beatrix nodded in agreement.

"Oh yes!," Mrs. Vandenberg called from near the front door. "Do bring them up. I so want to treasure them and my friend." She waved Mickey Smith up the walk, then held open the front door for her to carry them into the house.

Horace and Beatrix watched as the chief released the body, and the ambulance crew drove off to the hospital. "Looks like gown and glove time," Horace told her.

Beatrix shook her head. "Not this time. I was here when it happened. I cannot help with the autopsy because I am a contaminated woman."

"Well, that's a new one. Never thought of you as being contaminated, but I see your point." Horace pulled out his pipe and lit it. "Thunderation, you'd be a big help right now."

"Thank you. It would be inappropriate since I am also a witness to her death. You, Theo, and Dr. Landis have done hundred of autopsies. This one is no different. Even if I were not contaminated, Clarice and I must stay here until Chief Clarke dismisses us. Perhaps longer because I am sure he will want to question us at length."

"At least we will have plenty to talk about later on this evening," Horace told her before turning to speak to the chief. He winced into a grimace.

"Chief, it looks like you're going to be busy for a while. I'm sure you'll want to get the names and addresses, maybe the telephone numbers of all the women. Might be helpful to find out from them if any of the regulars didn't turn out for the tea-sipping. They might have heard if she had some medical condition, too. I don't envy you, and then having to look over the inside. Looks like you're in for a long session. Beatrix is going to stay here for a while, so if you need any.... I'll be at the hospital. Let me know if you need me. I'll let you know when we have something – *if* there is something."

"Do you think it's a coincidence, these two women dying so soon, you know, close together, like this?" the chief asked.

"I don't want to say anything, but I do know that even an honest man can draw four aces." Horace's comment left the chief scratching his head.

It was well into twilight when Horace returned home, and was comforted to see his family and Beatrix, waiting for him. "Where's Theo?" Clarice asked with a yawn.

"Fred and I dropped him off. My kid brother is dead tired," Horace yawned. "So am I, for that matter. One of us will drive you back to your place when you're ready." He reached for his pipe and pouch.

"And?" Beatrix asked.

Horace chuckled. "After a false start, the short version is a sudden heart attack, just like the last time. No blockage, no sign of previous heart damage. Same thing. Identical."

"What false start?" Clarice asked.

Beatrix echoed with the same question.

"Well, when we were ready to begin Dr. Landis said he could smell almonds, and that led Theo and me to suspect cyanide poisoning. They smell just alike..."

Beatrix's eyes widened and she put her hand over her mouth for a second. "Oh, Horace, that is my fault. I did not tell you that Mrs. Vandenberg served a Dutch pastry called bonkatstaaf or bankett for short. At least I think that is the answer. It is made of almonds. I am very, very sorry."

"Not to worry. You didn't have time and we had more things on our minds than the menu. We figured it out once we checked the stomach contents. Looks like she swallowed some of it almost whole. After that, we made good progress, saw the chief and gave him our report, and he's gone over to talk with Mrs. Vandenberg again.

"Meanwhile, Beatrix and Clarice, tell us what happened after we left with the body."

The two women looked at each other, and Beatrix motioned for Clarice to go first. "It wasn't long after you left that the chief wanted the two of us to change places, so Beatrix came inside and I went out to be interviewed along with the others."

"And, while I kept watch on the house to make sure that nothing was touched," Beatrix added. "it also gave me an opportunity to look at each of the downstairs rooms and everything in them."

Horace knew exactly what she meant: She had mentally recorded everything.

"Chief Clarke kept all of us there until he had finished interviewing everyone. After he took all our names and addresses he told us there was nothing more for us to see and to go home. I left, but Beatrix stayed on with the chief," Clarice concluded.

"Clarice, you must have been gone when the chief told Mrs. Vandenberg that she could not stay at her house because it was a crime scene. She was very displeased about being ordered out of her own home, so the chief gave her a choice of staying at a hotel in town or a cell at the jail," Beatrix smiled. "She chose the Butler."

"Wise choice, although I'd hate to be on duty at the front desk tonight. Nothing will be good enough for her," Clarice laughed.

"What about the house?" Horace asked.

"It's locked up tight, and the chief has a patrolman keeping watch. He would like you and me to join him to inspect the house after he arrives here," Beatrix added.

"Well, perhaps I should go home and look after Theo," Clarice said. "And before you ask, it's a beautiful evening and this is my favorite time of the day. I will enjoy the walk."

"And, if we're still here when Chief Clarke comes, then that's when we are leaving, too," Harriet told Phoebe. She turned back to Horace and Beatrix. "What I can't understand is why someone would want to murder dear Mrs. Gray. She never had a nasty word to say about anyone, and she is, well, that is, was, always helping someone. She's kind, not toxic like some of the other women."

"Toxic might not be the best choice of words at the moment," Clarice said. "Harriet, would you like Phoebe to stay with us this evening? That way, you could stay while the chief is here. You know more about Mrs. Gray than the rest of us."

"That might be a good idea," Harriet said. "Yes, Phoebe, you'll stay with your aunt and uncle tonight."

"Do I get a say about this? I feel like I'm getting tossed back and forth like a football," Phoebe objected.

"No, not really; and yes, you are," her mother said. "The quarter-back just handed off the ball to another player. And behave yourself tonight at Aunt Clarice's, young lady. Your Uncle Theo is already very tired."

"Phoebe, I am so happy. I just realized you will be our first real guest in our new home. That makes you first to sign our guest book," Clarice told her.

The girl was not impressed. Sitting in on the conversation with Chief Clarke, her grandfather, and Beatrix would be more fun. Better yet would be if Fred was present.

"What I can't figure out is how someone got the poison into her," the chief said when he sat down in Horace's study. "And you're sure it was the same type? Digitalis?"

"Absolutely," Horace said. "I can't tell you how she received it, but I can tell you she didn't ingest it. No sign of it in her stomach or esophagus."

The chief turned to Beatrix. "Look, I know you didn't think it was ethical to assist with the autopsy, and I'm real grateful you and Mrs.

Balfour stayed to help, but I won't have any objections if you have a look on our victim tomorrow. I want you there, in fact."

"Thank you," Beatrix said quietly.

"Tonight, let's walk over and take another look at Mrs. Vandenberg's house. We might see something we missed earlier. A clue, maybe," the chief said.

Harriet invited herself along.

"I just don not fathom it. Not a thing out of place. Every glass and plate and piece of silverware right where it was when the women left. Not a thing moved in the kitchen. Nothing washed up, some of the food still on the counters and not in the icebox. The chief had me box up the glass and other things from where Mrs. Gray was sitting to test for something poisonous, but everything else is in perfect order, just the way it was. It just does not make sense that a lot of nice older rich women would be killing each other off," Beatrix said as she surveyed Mrs. Vandenberg's main floor. "There is too much pain."

"What did you get out of the maid?" Horace asked the chief.

"Not a lot, except for one thing. She's one tough lady. Tough as a railroad spike. She's a Dutch girl, lives up in Holland, and she made the pastry. She said she made it herself at home and brought it down to Mrs. Vandenberg. Mrs. V had her cut it into pieces and put it on a silver tray and then put it on the side board in the dining room. Oh, and a thick slice of it to go into the ice box. I checked; it's still there. That's what she did, and didn't touch it after that...."

"And I watched Mrs. Gray take the last piece. Everyone could have had a square or two, but only she ... no, that is not right!" Beatrix said, interrupting herself. "We are assuming something – that the maid did it. No. She is one person who could not have done it.

You smelled almond in the morgue, and you thought it might be cyanide, but it was not. An examination of her stomach contents proved that she had quite a few pieces, and an examination of her heart proved it was a heart attack. So, that rules out the maid, and we are getting diverted by cyanide."

"I agree. And let's confirm with an analysis of the remaining pastry," Horace said.

"So that leaves everyone else as a suspect," Chief Clarke moaned. "We're back to square one again."

"Thunderation. We need to find a motive," Horace said.

"We need to find a motive. We do indeed," the chief repeated. "And it isn't likely to be tonight. I need to do some door checks and then go home and get some sleep. Tomorrow's another day. Goodnight, all. And Doctor Balfour, thank you for your help."

She nodded wearily in recognition of the compliment.

"I agree with you. Let's close up the place, and get some shut-eye," Horace told him.

"Before you go, Chief, I knew Mrs. Gray from Ox-Bow, and she was a wonderfully kind woman. There was something always sad about her. Nothing she would ever talk about, just sort of this heavy-heartedness. I can't explain it. But people liked her," Harriet said.

"That's good to know, and it makes this business all the more unpleasant. Come in tomorrow and we'll fill out a report," the chief said. "Goodnight, all, again."

Beatrix and Harriet walked back to Horace's house while he and the chief talked on the sidewalk. He was only a few minutes behind her, but by the time he returned the two women were already deep in a conversation. "I was just telling Beatrix that finding out anything from those women won't be easy. They have a code of silence that shrouds them, especially if it is anything unpleasant. They clam up and pretend everything is perfect in their lives. They want to keep it a secret from everyone, except sooner or later someone in their social set finds out, and then things get vicious," Harriet said. "They're tighter than Capone's code of amaretto."

"Harriet, I do not believe that is the right word. Amaretto is an alcoholic drink; the Chicago Mob have a code of omerta," Beatrix explained.

Harriet gave her a weary smile and ignored the correction.

"Let me ask you a question. What did the flowers on the table look like?" Harriet asked.

"They were beautiful. Perfect shape and color, and beautifully arranged," Beatrix said.

"Of course they were. Now, do you think they came from Mrs. Vandenberg's garden, and that she picked and arranged them herself?"

"No. Absolutely not. First, she wouldn't cut her own flowers because that would diminish her garden. And second, she certainly wouldn't want dirt under her fingernails, or take the time arranging flowers."

"Then where did the flowers come from?" Horace asked, joining the conversation.

Harriet sighed loudly. "Most people in town turn to the Flower Fairy. That's the name of Mickey Smith's flower shop. You must have met her today. She's expensive, and Mrs. Vandenberg is, well, basically cheap, but Miss Smith is very good. She's an artist when it comes to flowers. My guess is that she paid her maid a pittance to bring flowers from her home, then took them to the shop and told the Flower Fairy they came from her garden."

"Still, it would be worth finding out for certain," Horace said.

Beatrix was staring at the opposite wall, and slowly began adding, "And because they all have these secrets and pretend everything is perfect in their life, but others know their secrets and short-comings, they jab at each other like boxers. They make cutting comments instead of a physical punch, because none of them really wants to throw the knock-out punch." She looked up in horror, then looked down. "There is so much pain in the world, and they take delight in adding to it."

"It's competition, pure and simple, no messing," Harriet said.

"Competition, but for what reason?" Beatrix asked.

"Status." Harriet said lightly. "The perishable laurel wreath of status."

"And yet when they are gone, no one will care," Beatrix replied.

"That's because there will be a whole new generation to take their places. Well, I must be going. I know it sounds dreadful, but I am so looking forward to a long hot bath and a very quiet night alone. Thank goodness for Clarice. Goodnight, you two," Harriet said.

Horace and Beatrix sat in silence in Horace's study, and finally Horace slid the cigar humidor in her direction. "A humidor?" she asked. "A new acquisition."

"Keeps the cigars fresher that way. Considering how things are turning out, they won't be around long enough to get stale. Want to move out to the front porch?" he asked.

"Do you think that is a good idea; me smoking a cigar in public?" she asked.

"It's dark. I doubt anyone will even notice."

They sat some distance from each other in rocking chairs, facing the street. Beatrix began to relax a bit. "Do you think we're approaching this the right way?" she asked.

"What do you mean?"

"There are too many uncertainties. We know that Miss Stymington was murdered, but how can we be sure someone killed Mrs. Gray? Perhaps it was Mrs. Gray who did it, killed Miss Stymington, that is, and when she realized that her cause of death had been discovered she took her own life before she was arrested. That assumes that she was the murderer. Or, perhaps something else caused a sudden myocardial infarction," she suggested quietly.

"True enough. We examined every inch of Mrs. Gray's body for a puncture wound. Doc Landis thought maybe she's sat on a needle, but there was no wound, and no sign of a needle in her clothes."

Beatrix stifled a giggle by putting a hand over her mouth. "This is very impertinent, but Horace, I doubt a needle would have penetrated her foundation garments. They are called that for a very good reason. And in her case….."

"True. But from what Harriet and Clarice were saying, it's going to be just as difficult to penetrate this wall of silence and perfection."

Beatrix didn't say anything until she had knocked a long ash off the end of her cigar. "I can think of two back doors."

"What? Keep talking."

"There are two possibilities. The first is Mickey Smith, the florist. Harriet said that the women don't take flowers from their gardens, and probably does all of the arranging. If that is the case she has access to their homes, and if she has access to their homes, then she'll over-hear some of their secrets. If those women can't confide in each other, they might turn to her. And the second one is Bobbie at the telephone switchboard. She would know everything going on in this town."

"I like the idea. Both of them. But will Bobbie squeal on them?" Horace asked.

Horace couldn't see her smile when she said, "All it will take is a bit of flattery. That's your department."

"I think I'll give that assignment to Fred."

Horace tapped out his pipe, and Beatrix's cigar was short and the taste turning bitter. "I'll walk you home," he suggested.

"I am perfectly capable of finding my way around the corner," she said. She stood up, stretched for a moment, and was on her way.

It was an hour later and by then Horace was asleep when he heard something hitting his bedroom window. He lifted the window sash to see what was going on. "The atomizer is missing!" It was Beatrix standing on the driveway.

"The what?" he asked, not fully awake.

"The atomizer is missing!"

"Your atomizer?"

"No, Horace. The atomizer at Mrs. Vandenberg's home."

"What are you talking about?" he asked.

"When Clarice and I arrived there in the afternoon I went to the powder room to check my hair, and there was a perfume atomizer on the vanity. After Mrs. Gray died and I investigated the house, it was not there. I just realized it. We must investigate further in the morning. It may be important."

"Yeah, let's do that in the morning," Horace told her, stifling an intense yawn.

TEN

The latest edition of the *Commercial Record* had come out the night before, and it had sold so well the editor ordered another five hundred copies. "People'll want to hold on to it as a keepsake," he told Archie. "Now, go out there and peddle 'em so we don't lose money. Hire a couple of kids to sell them, and get them delivered to the stores." There was little chance of losing money on the second edition; everyone wanted at least one copy.

As Fred said later, "that there story is just about as lurid as anything written by Hearst back in the days of yellow journalism when McKinley was in the White House. Stories like that is how you get a war started if you're not careful about it." Miss Stymington was described as a society dame, a true matron of high culture and society with ancestors who stepped onto the rock in Plymouth, a member of the Colonial Dames of America, the Daughters of the American Revolution, and philanthropist. Her interest in spiritualism had led her to found the Heavenly Blessed Congregation on the outskirts of town, and she was highly knowledgeable in gardening and floral arranging.

"Think ol' Archie got paid by the inch?" Theo asked as he folded the newspaper and tossed it aside. "You know, it's moments like this when I kind of miss old Chief Garrison. He'd be lit up like a sky-rocket on the Fourth of July if he read that."

"And just as bombastic," Horace chuckled. "Thunderation, that man was explosive."

Theo suddenly became more serious. "Horace, Clarice and I were talking it over this morning, and I don't know how you feel about this since it's your practice. But, if you think it might help, I could fill in for you while you and Fred and Beatrix figure this thing out," he said, pointing to the newspaper.

"That's very kind," Horace said quietly. "I'll clear it with Landis, but I'm sure he ll agree to it. I appreciate it. We need to get this solved before another one happens, or before everyone gets spooked by their own shadow."

"So, you think it's a local doing it?"

"I'm certain of it. There's no question in my mind. So are Beatrix and Harriet. The only common denominator is that these two women have is they were both members of every social group in town and they were well-off. Even Phoebe is convinced of it, as well."

"And just how are you two and our chief going to solve it?"

"To start off, Beatrix is going to do some more work on the victim, Mrs. Gray. Somehow, the digitalis or some other toxin got into her body. She hopes to find it. You know, if things are quiet, you might be able to give her a hand."

"If she will tolerate it," Theo said.

"Then, early this afternoon Clarice is going to see Mrs. Vandenberg and offer condolences for the way her card party folded. If nothing else the visit will take her mind off having to stay away from her house for another day or so. Maybe your wife can pick up something useful for us. Right now, I'm about to go to have a little chat and see if I can learn anything from Bobbie over at the switchboard."

"I'm half surprised you didn't send Fred over to the flower shop to talk with Mickey Smith. She's in and out of every house and church around."

"I'm seeing her after I wrap things up with Bobbie."

"You might want to rethink that just a little. Fred's got a natural connection with her. Her husband was in the Marines during the war. He was gassed at Belau Woods."

"Really?" Horace asked. "I didn't know she was ever married. Good thing you told me. All right, we'll send Fred to see her. Oh wait! Beatrix..."

"What about her?"

"She woke me up in the middle of the night..." Horace started.

"Well, say now, that's something! Hope it doesn't get into the paper," Theo teased.

"No, not the way you think. She was outside on the driveway throwing pebbles at my window. She said that Mrs. Vandenberg's atomizer was missing from the powder room."

"She woke you up to tell you that, you said? She must think it's important," Theo said firmly. "She's a handful, but Beatrix is usually on the right track."

Horace made arrangements with Beatrix and the chief to meet at Mrs. Vandenberg's house at noon. That gave him time to walk down to the telephone office where he found Bobbie at the switchboard. "Busy day?" he asked.

"Not yet. Things heat up late in the morning and then for a couple of hours in the afternoon. Mornings, and it's calls to the stores and shops for orders, then it gets quiet until afternoon when the ladies start calling each other to chat. Is there something I can do for you?" Bobbie asked. She put down a Hollywood movie magazine.

"Yes. Yes, there is. I'm sure you read about Mrs. Stymington's death..."

"Yes, and now that dear, sweet Mrs. Gray. I feel so sorry for her."

"Why is that?" Horace asked.

Bobbie motioned to a chair, inviting Horace to sit down. "Well, for one thing, she was a widow. Her late husband was a high-up muckety-muck at the stockyards out in Nebraska before he died. That's what led her here to Saugatuck during the summers. She decided she wanted to try her hand at art, and went to Ox-Bow for classes and such-not. Well, after her husband passed, word got around that she was pretty well-healed, so all of a sudden she had a lot of friends. You know the type – women who haven't got enough to do in their life but play cards and have committee meetings.

"Anyway, she had a couple of her paintings in the art show down to the park. You know the one where they stretch out this clothesline between a couple of trees to hang their pictures on. Now, I heard that one year some of the women talked her into putting her paintings in the show, and then they turned right around and laughed behind her back about how she didn't have no talent. If she ever got wind of it, she kept it to herself. After that, I guess they sort of kept her around to make the rest of them feel better."

"What do you mean by that?" Horace asked.

Bobbie leaned closer to him and lowered her voice. "Well, they could pick on her and laugh at her behind her back. You know, they'd say things like 'at least I'm not as fat as Mrs. Gray,' or 'did you see the dress she was wearing yesterday?' in that nasty tone of voice. They gossip about everybody."

"That's rough," Horace said quietly, remembering Beatrix's words about too much pain in the world.

"Well, not none of us is perfect. It would have been one thing if someone had quietly said to her she might want to think about not eating all the time, or given a genuine idea how to improve a painting. None of them women would do that, mind you. They'd wait until they could stab her in the back, so to speak."

"What have you learned since Mrs. Stymington's murder?" Horace asked.

Bobbie sat up straight. "Now, you know I'm not allowed to repeat anything I hear. I'm not supposed to be listening in!"

"Oh, I know that," Horace said with a big smile, "but I'm helping out Chief Clarke with the investigation, and Bobbie, I'll let you in on something. Mrs. Gray's death is listed as suspicious. Right now, Doctor Howell is looking for a cause of death. Now, if Mrs. Gray was murdered, others might be in danger. If you'll bend the rules just a bit, just a little, you might help save someone else from getting killed."

Bobbie thought over his request, then raised her right hand before putting it over her heart. "I swear I haven't heard anything yet. Sure, they're all talking about Miss Stymington and what a great woman she was and how she did so much for Saugatuck, but that's the way some of them are whenever anyone dies. So, I'll tell you what, if I hear anything that might be helpful, I'll let you know. I promise! That good enough?"

Horace smiled. "That would be a tremendous help, and a real service to all of us, Bobbie. Thank you."

"Doc," Bobbie said as he was about to leave. "I sure hope your grand daughter doesn't grow up to be one of them. I don't think she will, but it's got to be a worry for Harriet. And for you."

Horace left the Maplewood Hotel and walked to the park, to sit a bench, smoke his pipe, and think things over. "Want to buy some flowers, Mister?" a voice asked.

"Phoebs, those are the same words you said when we first met!" Horace was all smiles at the sight of his granddaughter. "That brings back some pretty good memories!"

"And memories of our first detective case, too. You're working on who rubbed out Miss Stymington and Mrs. Gray this time 'round. I'll bet it is a three-pipe problem!"

"Rubbed out? Phoebe! Are you thinking about being a double agent or becoming a moll for a mobster or something?" They both laughed. "I'll tell you one thing though, you'd better not let your mother hear you use those words. What are you doing this morning?"

"I'm waiting for the library to open. But that can wait if you need a right-hand girl," she offered.

"I do. Here's the thing. I'm hearing the same old story over and over. I need to know if there is more. You got any ideas of someone I could interview? And maybe you can get a couple of your friends to squeal on what they overheard from their mother about Miss Stymington or Mrs. Gray."

"Of course! You should talk to Whistlin' Bill!" she said brightly.

"Who in the world is Whistlin' Bill?"

"You must have seen him around. He works around town as a handyman, and he knows everyone, and he whistles and plays the accordion. If anyone one has picked up any news it would be old Whistlin' Bill because everyone likes him so they talk to him. People like to have someone who listens to them."

"That's a keen observation, Phoebe. Now, where do we find your friend Whistlin' Bill?"

"Oh, I'd say if we sit right here and think about him, he'll turn up in about a minute or less," she teased. She smiled at her grandfather's confusion, then pointed down Butler Street. "That's him coming our way." He had a smile on his face when he saw Phoebe and Doctor Balfour.

Whistlin' Bill didn't have much to add. He repeated just about everything that had already been said – like most society women Miss Stymington was snooty and cheap. "Sometimes I'll be sitting right here on this very bench playing my accordion and my hat out. Lots of folks will put in a nickel or a dime, sometimes more, but she and her bunch would walk right past as if I am completely invisible. Tell you the truth, Doc, I wish I did had some dirt on her just to give her what-for."

Horace took the hint, and pulled out a dollar bill. "You've been a lot of help."

"Sure do wish I had some dirt on her to earn this," he said staring at the bill. "Nah, I like to think that way sometimes, but I wouldn't want to do it. I wouldn't feel good about myself if I was that way."

"Tell you what, you hear anything and I'll make it worth your while."

"I'm confident you will. You look like the man who keeps his word," Whistlin' Bill said. As the fellow walked off Horace realized that he'd been in Saugatuck for several years and their paths had never crossed. He shivered, realizing that perhaps he had seen him before, but never spoke to him.

"Phoebs, I've got to get up to Mrs. Vandenberg's house," Horace told her.

"I'd better come along with you, just in case you need me."

"That will be fine, but the chief might not let you in, you know."

"That's jake with me because he just might let me come inside. If he doesn't, then I'll go to the library."

"When we are finished I must talk with you," Beatrix whispered to Horace as they waited for the chief. "Not now," she added, nodding toward the street as the chief pulled up.

"What do we hope to find?" Chief Clarke asked.

"Evidence," Beatrix said. "I just don't know what we need to find. Chief, please tell me that you secured Mrs. Gray's house to preserve evidence there."

"Well, ah, it's like this Doctor. We're a little short handed. I got a police department of three. One man has been here all night, Dwight's resting, and then there's me."

"That is not good," Beatrix said worriedly. She looked at Horace, and Horace turned to Phoebe.

"You have an assignment. I want you to find Fred. Start by checking his apartment. If he isn't there, drive through town, keep your eyes open, and go over to the Flower Fairy shop and see if he is there or at the hospital. Just find him and take him to Mrs. Gray's house. Tell him to defend the house until relieved. He'll know what that means."

" Defend the house until relieved. Understood," Phoebe told her. "Grandfather, do you know where Mrs. Gray lived? I really should have an address."

Horace turned to the chief who hemmed and hawed about. "Well, she lives sort of across the street from the first preacher at the Episcopal Church. It's a big house up on the bluff.. You can't miss it. Lots of gables and gingerbread. That's where the preacher lived, and Mrs. Gray lived across the street."

"Thank you," Phoebe said cautiously. "Oh, and chief, can I borrow your car? I'm on foot."

"No!" he snapped.

"Take mine. It's simple to drive. There is a toggle switch to turn on the battery to your left, and a brass plate with operating instructions on the dashboard to your right. I would suggest you read it carefully. And, do be careful. The batteries are fully charged so the car can be very sprightly."

Phoebe's eyes widened. Doctor Howell was loaning her Detroit Electric. She had ridden in it before, and knew how the car worked. The big danger was that it was so slow she was likely to be rear-ended by another car. The only thing worse than getting killed while driving it was the chance one of her friends would see her in such an ugly vehicle.

It didn't take her long to spot her grandfather's car. Fred was just getting out of it in front of the flower shop. She squeezed the rubber ball to make the horn give an anemic sound like a flatulent cow.

"Guard the house until relieved. Got the message. Tell your grandfather the general I got his orders," Guess I'd better take along this here equalizer Doc keeps under the dash, just in case there's any trouble. The boss didn't say nothing about a password, did he? Or maybe when the relief column should be coming up the line?"

"No, Fred. All he said was to find you, tell you to guard the house until relieved. I've got to go and get that car back to Doctor Howell before someone sees me in it. My life will be ruined if anyone seems me driving that thing."

"Doctor Howell, is there anything we're looking for in particular?" the chief asked once they were inside Mrs. Vandenberg's house.

"Yes, a small square clear glass bottle for perfume, without a label on it. It is an atomizer. There is a lime green rubber ball on a short hose. If you see it, be careful to preserve any fingerprints, and for heaven's sake, do not squeeze the bulb. Chief, please check the kitchen for it, especially the backs of any cabinets or drawers. Horace, the upstairs bedroom, starting with the nightstand and a bureau. I will look at the powder room and then the bathroom upstairs."

"Why are we looking for it?" the chief asked.

"Because it was in the powder room earlier in the afternoon, and it wasn't there after Mrs. Gray's death," Horace told him as they went up the stairs. "That's all I know, and it's good enough for me."

"How come we're so certain it was there in the first place?" the chief asked.

"Because Doctor Howell said so."

Even after a diligent search, and all three of them shifting rooms in hopes that one might see what the other two had missed, they had not found the atomizer. "Are you..." the chief started to ask Beatrix.

"If she said she saw it, she saw it. We aren't finding it now because it isn't here," Horace said quickly and grimly.

"Perhaps Mrs. Vandenberg took it with her," the chief said.

"That is highly doubtful, but it would be prudent to ask," Beatrix said. "Clarice is with her now at the Butler. Our next stop, perhaps?

"Our next stop," Horace said.

Horace and Beatrix found a rare empty parking spot near the Butler Hotel, then hurried up the steps. Just as they were about to go into the lobby Horace heard someone whistle and call his name. It was Whistlin' Bill, sitting on a straight back chair, playing his accordion.

"I will go up alone. Mrs. Vandenberg might be more forthcoming if you are not present when we ask her about the perfume," Beatrix said.

Horace nodded in agreement and went over to where Whistlin' Bill was sitting. "Glad I ran across you again," he said, putting down his instrument. "I didn't want to talk too much when young Miss Phoebe was there, seeing that she's a youngster and all." He looked around to make sure no one was listening. "This doesn't sound very nice, but like I said earlier, some of those women can be pretty rough on each other, real rough and nasty. When I was a tyke my mother would sometimes take me along to her church ladies aid meetings, and I saw the same thing back then. Back then we thought people were nicer and more polite to one another than they are sometimes nowadays. At least it seemed that way, but maybe it ain't so. People is still people."

Horace smiled and nodded in agreement.

"Are you and your lady going to Miss Stymington's funeral tomorrow?"

"Doctor Howell and I were planning on it, yes. Is there something we should know?" Horace asked.

"Well, it's not my place to tell a man of your station what to do, but I'd sure encourage you to stay on for the eats down in the basement."

"You think someone's going to try slipping something into the food?" Horace asked, alarmed.

"I doubt it. Now, I'm no Sherlock Holmes, but I doubt it. It would be too easy to trace back to them. No, what you want to do is watch what's going on in the kitchen. Forget what's going on in the dining room unless a ruckus gets started; it's the kitchen you want to keep watch on. You wanted to know what some of those women were like. Now, just some of them, don't get me wrong. Not all of them. You take a look at them out there in the dining hall and then you see them back in the kitchen. Before long they'll be edging toward the drawers with the big knives in it. Or maybe one of 'em will hold a big soup ladle, just in case she has to wallop another one of them. They won't get the knives out or anything, but they'll sort of make like they're not afraid of a good scrape and dust-up." He nodded, suddenly picking up his accordion because he saw someone coming near them. "Maybe I'll catch up with you tomorrow. And say, thank you. That sure was a generous tip."

Horace took the hint and reached in his pocket for a handful of change.

ELEVEN

"Anything? Any news?" Horace asked when Beatrix came down from Mrs. Vandenberg's room?

"She opened up her handbag and her grip to show us. Nothing," Beatrix said. "It means nothing. If she owned the bottle, she could have easily disposed of it. If she took it with her when she moved to the Butler, it could be in the town dump by now.

"Well, at least we know."

"Horace, we are getting out in front of ourselves. I have news from the lab I have not had an opportunity to tell you, and no doubt you have new intelligence you have collected. I propose we go somewhere and talk."

"Say, I've got an idea! How about we stop in at Parrish's drugstore for..."

Beatrix cut him off. "It is too early in the day for ice cream And before even you suggest it, the answer is 'no' to a Green River. Perhaps a root beer. I will even go so far as a root beer float."

After they sat down, Beatrix said. "I have not told you about this morning in the lab. You were right about the digitalis. She was poisoned. That is why I need to find the perfume atomizer."

Horace was stunned by the news, and for several seconds stared at her before muttering, "Thunderation! You mean she accidently killed herself?"

"Yes. Someone, very likely someone other than Mrs. Gray, must have placed the atomizer with the digitalis on the vanity in the powder room. It is uncharitable to say this, but the woman could be very greedy. As I said, we all saw her snitch the last of the dessert, and it wasn't the first time she has done it. She did it all the time. I believe that she went into the powder room, saw the atomizer and could not resist spraying on her face what she assumed was perfume."

"A fatal error," Horace said quietly. "Greed truly is one of the seven deadly sins."

"Indeed. Theo and I found traces of it on her face, neck, and behind her ears. She practically bathed in it, perhaps because it does not have much of a scent. She apparently sprayed a considerable amount, The interesting thing is that there are other people complain about the way foxglove smells."

"Not much of a scent, so she used more. Tragic. Again, remembering the atomizer is why I woke you in the middle of the night, and why we still need to find it."

"It may be far too late for that. Like you just said, for all we know, whoever brought it has tossed it away and its in the city dump," Horace said gloomily. "And even if we did find it, the chances of fingerprints are pretty small."

"What did you learn?" Beatrix asked, abruptly changing the subject.

"Plenty. The general news is that Miss Stymington's funeral is tomorrow. I heard that from a couple of people. Then Phoebs introduced me to an interesting local character who goes by the name of Whistlin' Bill. He said it might be helpful to go to the funeral and the reception, especially the reception."

"I think going to the funeral is advisable, but please, not a social *do* in a church basement," Beatrix said.

"Why?"

"Very simply, it will be too noisy, too crowded with people bumping into each other, many of them trying to get to the reception line before anyone else, and truly bad food. Others will be crowding behind them, hurrying them along. My guess is that it will be ham buns, thin slices of ham, ham salad, and cookies," she said with disdain and ended with a shudder. "Oh, and pickles."

"Research, Beatrix, research," Horace told her. She said nothing, but tightened her lips.

"I take it you don't much care for pickles?" he asked.

"They are cucumbers corrupted by vinegar," she said firmly.

Beatrix, Horace, Theo, and Clarice all arrived at the Church of the Heavenly Blessed just in time to watch Mickey Smith unload more flowers from her van, with three employees trailing behind, all carrying floral arrangements. "Thunderation, I thought only Capone and company were this lavish with flowers," Horace growled under his breath.

"Behave or I'm going to send you right back home," his brother teased.

"Promise?"

"But you are right, it is ostentatious, is it not?" Beatrix asked as they walked up the sidewalk and joined the others signing the registry. She grimaced as they went into the church, and nearly turned around at the sound of so many people, all trying to be heard over the others. "I think perhaps I can do more good watching for anything outside," she said. "At least there it will be quiet."

"I agree. I'll help you keep watch and then we'll slip down to the church hall just before the last hymn," Horace told her.

They found a bench in the small garden where they could watch the back door leading into the basement. "If there is any funny business going on, it will be back here," Horace said.

"Oh, do you really think anyone will be laughing at a funeral?" Beatrix asked seriously.

"Probably not. I meant something nefarious."

"Oh. Yes, of course."

From their seat they could hear the funeral service begin with soloist singing *Amazing Grace*. Horace winced, "Seems like all the geriatric sopranos are vying with each other to be the loudest."

"And most off key," Beatrix added. "This is very painful to hear," as they suffered through three verses. "It gives a new meaning to the word 'rendering,' does it not?" She nodded towards the back door. "Quite a bit of activity, is there not? I would have thought they all would be upstairs at the funeral."

"Not when there is work to be done. Let's take a look." They silently padded down the steps, standing on the final step, listening.

Mrs. Vandenberg and two other women were in the kitchen, dressed for the funeral and reception, Mrs. Vandenberg wearing what Horace's mother would have called her "fancy apron" that was more for show than practicality. All three were having a heated discussion, standing close to a large preparation table.

"Mrs. Vandenberg, this is not your church and this is not your kitchen," Mrs. Zimmerman said firmly. "Mrs. Starmer and I have been members ever since it was founded, and we are perfectly capable of handling a funeral reception. Now, if you can't keep quiet, then get out."

"All I was trying to suggest is that there is a more elegant way of presenting the refreshments. I would have thought you wanted to make a good impression," Mrs. Vandenberg said icily. "Miss Stymington was a very good friend an important woman in our community."

"Mrs. Zimmerman is right," added Mrs. Starmer quietly. "This really is not your kitchen, and we have our own traditions." She force a smile onto her face. "We know what we are doing, thank you very much!"

Mrs. Vandenberg's hands were on her hips, and she pulled herself up a bit taller. "Well, as I just told you, Miss Stymington was an important mem..."

Mrs. Zimmerman cut her off. "In this house of worship, we believe everyone, every single person, is important. They're important to the community, and they are equally important in the eyes of God, which is something you would have heard if you had ever bothered yourself to come to church here!"

"Oh yes, now let's bring God into a funeral service! Your attitude is rather Bolshie, don't you think. Everyone being equal and all that. Do you call each other 'Comrade'?"

"If you don't like how we do things here, then I suggest you just march yourself out the door and go back to Evanston or wherever it is you came from!" Mrs. Zimmerman snapped. Seeing a large spoon for mixing the punch, she picked it up and held it, ready to strike her nemesis.

"Evanston? Hardly dear. Lake Forest, where we know the right way to do things."

Mrs. Zimmerman held the ladle a bit higher, menacingly. "Out! Now! Get out!"

"Well!"

Horace and Beatrix had to scramble up the stairs to avoid being seen. They trotted quickly back to their bench, just seated again and stifling a nervous giggle, when Mrs. Vandenberg came up the stairs, her face red with fury.

"I would not prescribe digitalis right now," Beatrix said quietly.

"I agree. For any of them. Not much love among the church kitchen ladies, is there?"

Beatrix turned to Horace and asked, "Do you think they are possible suspects?

Horace pulled out his pipe and slowly filled it, then fumbled through his pockets for his box of matches. He ignored Beatrix' question about the propriety of smoking a pipe on church property, and finally said, "Maybe. It might be easy enough for any of them to have killed Miss Stymington, but it's hard to figure out how they might have done in Mrs. Gray. Still, it is worth considering." Horace looked around to be sure no one was close or watching, then handed Beatrix his pipe.

The funeral took nearly an hour, due in great part because of a few eulogies and a very long-winded sermon. When a few people began leaving the church, Horace and Beatrix returned and went down the steps into the kitchen. They paused for a moment, noticing that the atmosphere was entirely different. Mrs. Zimmerman and Mrs. Starmer were supervising several churchwomen who were scurrying to keep the coffee urns filled and the platters supplied.

"Oh! Doctors!" Mrs. Starmer gasped in horror. "You've come through the back door."

"Well, I never stood on a lot of ceremony. Sort of reminds me of the time a colleague couldn't find the front door of a hospital he was visiting and came in through the back – right into the kitchen, just like we did today," Horace said.

"Doctor Landis did that?" she asked.

"No, it was someone else a few years back."

"Well, it's quite all right. I mean, you caught us in our aprons and up to our elbows in dishwater. But, welcome!" she replied. "Why don't you just slip in near the front of the line?"

"We'll wait our turn," he answered.

"Horace, it is very noisy and crowded in here," Beatrix said, her head down.

"I know. We need to remember we're looking for clues."

"Do we know what we are looking for?" She paused, looking stricken, then asked, "I should have said, 'do you know for what we are looking?'"

"Not exactly, but I think I spotted it at that table in the far corner. Mrs. Vandenberg and her cronies. From the way they keeping looking around, I'm certain they are discussing the women in the kitchen. Look, they know you, Beatrix. How about walking over there, sort of round about, while I keep an eye on them. I want to see how soon they notice you and then respond. I think once you talk with them you can come straight back here."

"Fine," she spat out. "Anything to get out of here all the sooner. I will go along the back wall and then along the side. But then I really must get away from here, Horace."

"I understand. Please don't rush or it will look like you are on an errand. Keep it casual. We'll get out of here in a few minutes," Horace reassured her.

Seven minutes later they were back outside and Beatrix's breathing slowed to a normal rate. "I am surprised you are not lighting your pipe," she said to him.

"And I shouldn't be surprised if you reached to borrow it, should I?" he asked, taking it out of his pocket. "Already to be lit; prime and loaded," he laughed gently.

She ignored him and asked what he had observed. "They definitely shifted around in their chairs when you approached, and I suspect they changed the topic of conversation. Something is up with them. Did you find out anything when you stopped at their table?"

"By the time I got close enough, they were talking about an upcoming flower show," Beatrix said.

"I think you were right, adding those two women in the kitchen to the list of possible suspects," Horace said quiet. "They might not be the only ones."

"You wanta know something, Boss? I can't figure out why you wanted to put in a flower bed. You've never been one for flowers and such, and I can't quite see you out there pulling weeds. You'd be further ahead if you'd just made it all grass," Fred said to him.

"You have a point there. And you're not much of a gardener, either, are you?" Horace asked with a smile.

"Nope. Never had been. Growing up, my folks had a garden, like they all did back then, and they always conscripted my brother and me to work it. Never liked doing it ever since," Fred said. "Course, if you were to give me an order to get out there in that hot sun and with all those chiggers and mosquitoes to weed it, I'd do it."

"And I appreciate your loyalty, sergeant."

"Now, what I was thinking is that there's this here young fellow here in town I know who'd do it for you cheap. See, people think he's either a little simple or tetched in the head, but he does a good job, and he could probably use the work," Fred suggested.

"Hire him," Horace said. "The sooner the better."

"I kinda thought you'd say that. Now, I'll see if I can find him. He's probably working somewhere today and his truck isn't hard to spot. And see, here's what makes folks think he's tetched...."

Horace cut him off. "Fred, you've talked me into it. Just go find him, hire him, and get him over here to prettify the place." He turned to walk into his house.

MURDER OF THE SAUGATUCK CHURCH BASEMENT KITCHEN LADIES

TWELVE

Horace and Beatrix stopped at the police station early the next morning to see the chief. "Any progress? Horace asked.

"Well, I've talked to a lot of people and heard plenty, but I don't think it's getting me anywhere. I guess you must have heard by now that some of those women may be all lovey-dovey on the outside when others are watching, but alone, they sure do have the knives out for each other," Chief Clarke said.

Horace smiled and ran his hand across his chin. "Yeah that's what I get too."

"As well as big metal spoons," Beatrix added. "We saw that yesterday when some of them were in the midst of a heated discussion."

The chief nodded in agreement although he had no idea what she meant. "I asked my mother why that is. I mean, a couple of fellows have a beef and we'll duke it out or worse...."

Horace laughed and interrupted. "We use to settle it behind the livery stable until Old Jensen came out, pitchfork in hand, and told us to get moving, I don't think many punches landed; just a lot of posturing and circling round."

The chief continued, "But that's not how these women behave. They're more manipulative. They keep needling each other, picking at one another. And Ma said it's because some of them are repressed. You know, not having the vote, not having a job unless it was being a teacher or a nurse, and then they had to quit when they got married or in the family way, if you know what I mean. I didn't know it growing up, but she said that Pa gave her an allowance for the house and food. He went over the accounts at the end of every month. I guess things like that might have something to do with them taking it out on each other."

"There might be something to it. You figure that's what caused this?" Horace asked.

"Maybe. I was talking to the minister at her church and he said that the Sunday before Miss Stymington was killed she was in a right snit. See, she had charge of the flowers, and someone brought in some flowers that she hadn't ordered, and she took it as someone cutting in on her territory. Plus, it had some strange flower in it that I've never seen before. A big orange flower that looks like it comes from outer space. Well, she didn't like it, not one bit, she didn't, and from what he said, she made her thoughts known loud and clear."

"Do you know what it was called?" Beatrix asked.

The chief chuckled, "Well, that's the puzzler. This ugly flower is called a Bird of Paradise."

"Aside from it being strange-looking what got her stirred up? Because she didn't pick it out?" Horace asked.

"Not exactly, although that's probably part of it. No, the minister said that she didn't like it because she thought it was some sort of harbinger of death. That doesn't make any sense to me. But he said that it was in the sanctuary right in front of the altar and she took it out of there and put it in the kitchen to get rid of it. She was pretty hot about it, from what he said."

Horace closed his eyes for a moment, reviewing the kitchen in his mind. "I don't recall seeing it in the kitchen when we found her body."

"Nor I," Beatrix echoed.

"Neither did I. So, I asked the minister if he'd seen it, and he said he hadn't seen it after Sunday morning. He thought maybe someone took it home, but I didn't take any chances, so I checked the trash cans out in back, and it wasn't there. It doesn't make any sense to me and maybe it doesn't have anything to do with her murder."

"Probably not," Beatrix agreed. "What about Mrs. Gray? What have you learned about her?"

"Well, she was different, entirely different. Everyone said she was nice and kind but didn't really fit in. I got hold of her son in New York City, and he said he was sending an obituary to the paper. I figure it won't get here for a couple of days so I asked him to tell me what he wrote. Long story short, she was born and grew up in eastern Nebraska and went to a little Methodist college in Sioux City for two to become a teacher, and that's where she met her husband. She taught for a year and then got married, and he was a big wheel at the stockyards in South Sioux City over in Nebraska. That's where he made his money and he did okay for themselves. They had the one son, oh, and a daughter who died in 1918 of the Spanish Flu. My guess is that he'll inherit everything. I can't see how he could have anything to do with his mother's murder, can you?"

"Not if he was in New York at the time. No. When he gets here for the wake I'll be sure he was in New York. The thing is, both of them died because of these fox glove plants. I've got half a mind to ask the village council to outlaw growing poisonous flowers."

"I see your point, but from what Doctor Howell tells me, about half the plants in anyone's garden are toxic. You won't get too far with that one."

"I believe many of the members of the Garden Tea society will strenuously object," Beatrix added.

The chief's eyes widened. "Last thing I need right now is a delegation of club women in here fussing about outlawing anything poisonous in their gardens."

"I believe that is a very good observation Chief," Beatrix said. "Gentlemen, I must go to the hospital. Doctor Theo Balfour is examining a patient with a leg sore that will not heal. He has asked me to run some blood tests."

She got up to leave, then stopped at the door to turn around. "By the way chief, in addition to foxglove and flower hemlock being poisonous, you could include tomatoes, peppers, and cucumbers. They are all part of the nightshade family. If you pursue a plan to outlaw the poisonous plants you will also anger many others."

When Horace left the police station he walked a couple of blocks over to the Flower Fairy shop to talk with Mickey Smith, the owner. She seemed flustered when she came out of the back room, pulling the door shut with a loud bang. After the usual small talk about the weather, the large turnout for Miss Stymington's funeral, and the work she had to do in preparation for Miss Gray's services, Horace asked her about the plant that had set off Miss Stymington just before she died. "Harbinger of death, I heard it called." He told her.

Mrs. Smith laughed. "That was a strange one. I've never heard it called that before, but I've seen it a few times. I got a letter in the mail with a five dollar bill asking me to deliver a Bird in Paradise stalk and bloom to her church, with her name on it. They *are* exotic, aren't they?"

"That happens often?" Horace asked. "I mean an order like that with money but no name of who sent it."

"Not exactly often, but it's not unusual. Usually it is some love-struck man sending a flower to a woman and he doesn't want to risk getting rejected. Anyway, I special ordered one from my wholesaler in Chicago and I did like the letter asked, and took it over to the church with the other arrangements. I guess the miserable shrew didn't like it. Sunday afternoon she called me, screeching like a mother blue jay when a cat gets too near the nest. I tried to explain things, but she just kept going at me."

"Did you go pick it up on Monday?" he asked.

"After the way she yelled at me, not on your nelly! It could stay there until the petals fall off, for all I cared!" Miss Smith said.

"I see."

"You want to know something, Doctor Balfour, I'm getting tired of this job. It isn't just her or because she chewed me out. After a while it gets old and boring. It gets to me. I get orders for all sorts of functions or no special occasions, and it's always the same – roses, tulips, carnations, and flowers like that. Iris in the spring, daffodils. Nothing creative, nothing interesting or special." She leaned closer and looked around, "And you want to know something? The worst of them are the Garden and Tea Club members. You'd think they'd like to be creative, adventurous, but no, not them, the same old stuff year after year. And they can be cheap, sometimes. Nothing out of season because that might cost them too much. Like I said, I'm getting bored with this line of work."

"I understand all that. But here's what I don't understand. If Miss Stymington hated those bird of paradise flowers, why would there be several arrangements of them at the reception?" Horace asked.

"Pure spite, that's why. You must have heard by now that she was envied, feared, even appreciated for all she did, but no one loved her. They hated her. That's not nice to say, but it's the truth. I had three orders for those flowers for her reception. Can you believe it?

An expensive way to show contempt, wouldn't you say?" Mrs. Smith asked.

"I know. I saw them there. It might help solving who killed her if you could tell me who sent the flowers," Horace suggested gently.

"Well, then you and I would both know. All I know is that I got three letters, three five dollar bills, and three messages to get bird of Paradise," Mickey said tiredly.

"By any chance did you keep the envelopes?"

Mickey slowly turned completely around, a finger pointing as she turned, and said, "Look at this place. It looks like a cyclone swept through Bedlam. I've been run off my feet. The place is a mess right now. So, where do you think I kept envelopes? You can look for them and help clean up at the same time."

Horace looked at the shop – overflowing waste paper baskets, clipped and cut leaves and small branches on the floor, the work bench with more debris. The only clean surface was a small portion of the workbench where a stretched out cat was working his tail back and forth. "I see your point," he said softly.

"I'd better get on my way so you can get to work. Any bird of paradise flowers for Mrs. Grey?" Horace asked.

"Nah, people liked her, even if some of the old biddies were rough on her."

There was a different mood at Mrs. Gray's funeral. Clarice and Beatrix sat with the other women who had been at Mrs. Van-denberg's house when she died. "A show of solidarity," Clarice explained. Theo, Harriet, and Horace sat a few rows back in the old church. Not surprisingly, some of the same women spoke a second time that week of "our wonderful, dear, dear, sweet, talented

Mrs. Gray, who we all loved and cherished." She was followed by another acquaintance who said she was so grateful to the way Mrs. Gray appreciated the refreshments others had made. A soft twitter of laughter followed. A third spoke at length about her amateur art career, comparing her to the abstract and impressionistic artists of an earlier era, and concluding with the grandiose belief that everyone was inspired by her.

"Putting it on a bit thick, wouldn't you say, Harriet?" Horace whispered to her.

"It's nauseating. If lightning strikes them I am glad we're sitting in the back," she whispered in his ear.

At long last the casket was wheeled out of the church, followed by her son Clarence, his wife and their children. The mourners followed behind and went into the church hall for the reception. "I am leaving, Horace," Harriet said. "I have had enough clichés and hypocrisy for one day. It is almost word for word what they said at the last funeral; just a different name. Horace nodded in agreement and walked out with her.

"All a bit sad, isn't it?" he asked her, not certain if it was the right thing to say. "I'll bet the pulpit pounders repeat funeral sermons, too." He chuckled, adding, "Wonder if they ever get the wrong name?"

"It is sad. It really is. I looked at who was there. A couple of rows in front of us were two neighbors on my street. There was old Mr. Venno who used to teach math at the high school. He was a brutal tyrant. Next to him was my next door neighbor, Miss Reed. She is forever looking out her window keeping track of everything anyone does, and he's just as bad. You could see her shadow or see the curtains move, always snooping to see if it was a man calling at the door, or if I was going out for an evening. She's still at it. Trust me, she knows when you come up the walk. The old curtain twitcher and window peeker," Harriet said in disgust. "They're not the only ones holding grudges."

She continued, "Now, sometime just after the Civil War her mother dropped Mrs. Jordan's grandmother's pie plate. Mrs. Reed still claims it was an accident and her mother apologized and offered to buy her a new one. But Mrs. Jordan's mother claimed she did it out of spite and stuck by her story. Would you believe their daughters are still carrying on the feud and haven't spoken to each other since they were in school together. It goes on and on. No wonder there have been two murders! It's gotten to the point where they're killing each other, actually killing their rivals."

"I was beginning to think it was the clergy murdering each other's worst members," Horace teased gently. "You know, I'll get rid of your nemesis if you'll return the favor. It might make for a pretty good racket."

"Them, too!" Harriet spat out, paused, and then smiled. "I'm sorry. That was wicked. I'm just not in a very good mood lately. Maybe I'm a little scared there is a killer on the loose, or maybe it's because... oh, I don't know. Horace, you and Beatrix have got to find who is doing this."

"We tried charting it out last night to make some sense. All we've got is digitalis and some older women who have died, well, been killed. But we can't find a motive."

"Money and family are usually the reasons," Harriet reminded him.

"Yes. And right now there isn't any indication it was that, either. Even their personalities were different. Miss Stymington was shrill, demanding, and not very likeable because of her caustic tongue. She gave orders but she'd never lift a hand to really do some work. Mrs. Grey was kind and harmless, and she was always the last to leave somewhere and always offered to help with the clean up. The only thing they had in common was that they were rich enough to have time for all these social groups and committees."

"There's something more, Horace. I may be talking out of turn, but I don't want Phoebe to have that life."

"No one would. Why would she?"

"If she thought she didn't have to go to college and work for a living she might end up just like them," Harriet said quietly.

"Then let's make sure that doesn't happen," he promised. "Look, I'm going back in and then walk home with Beatrix. Maybe she saw something or heard something."

"Put an end to this terror," Harriet told him firmly.

"Doing my best."

THIRTEEN

"Not eating anything?" Horace asked Beatrix when he found her near the back wall of the parish hall. She gave him a withering look. "Then, how about we get our skates on and go over to the drug store for a Coney?" he suggested.

"As long as you promise not to suggest a Green River once we get there," she said flatly. One look at her and Horace could see she was in pain from the noise and movement.

"Promise," he told her.

They had no more than sat down at one of the little round tables when Chief Clarke came in. "Room for one more?" he asked with a smile, as he sat before waiting for an answer.

"You look like a man who just solved a major crime," Horace said.

"Nah, not yet. Something even better. I'm seeing some friendly, familiar faces. You got any idea about the amount of grief I'm getting about not solving those two murders right away? Let's just say some of them are absolutely testy about it."

"They are scared, and perhaps for good reason," Beatrix said. "Frightened people often attempt to mask their fears by lashing out in anger."

"My question to you two is whether or not you've made any progress?" the chief asked.

Beatrix shook her head and looked down at the table.

"Maybe. I had some time to think this afternoon...," Horace started to say.

"I thought you went to Mrs. Gray's funeral," the chief objected.

"I did, and I've learned to do some of my best thinking during long-winded sermons. It keeps me from just sitting in the waiting room," Horace answered.

"Or snoring," Beatrix added, flashing a quick smile.

"Thunderation!" Horace retorted.

The chief looked puzzled at the comment about a waiting room, and was about to say something when Beatrix looked up and said, "Do not ask."

"I was thinking over a few things my daughter-in-law, Harriet Waters, said, and also my brother's wife. They both said that Mrs. Gray was generally the last person to leave any party or do. Most of the others thought it was so she could snitch something more to eat, and they'd laugh at her behind her back on account of it. But the two of them think the real reason was she was lonely and thought that if she helped out, people would like her better. Then again, maybe that's the way she was raised, and later on the money never changed her.

"The coffee party at Mrs. Vandenberg's house was different and ended unexpectedly after she took that telephone call from Archie from the Commercial Record. Beatrix, you and Clarice said that Mrs. Vandenberg came back into the room and stunned everyone with the news about Miss Stymington. The party fell apart after that, and everyone went home early."

The chief nodded in agreement. "I guess I didn't know much about her personality."

Horace continued, "By then, Mrs. Gray knew she wasn't feeling well. Clarice noticed it; perhaps some others did too, and just chalked it up to the bad news. This time, she left the party early. But she didn't want them to think she was rushing out the door. Maybe she was being polite, maybe she was distressed that if she was the first to leave others would make some cutting remarks. As it turned out, it was a good thing. She had a heart attack and died on the front walk, rather than rushing out the door, getting in her car, and maybe killing someone on the street."

"Okay, Doc, but where are you heading with all of this?" the chief asked.

Beatrix jumped in. "In short, she was poisoned while she was in Mrs. Vandenberg's house. She was killed by a lethal dose of digitalis while she was in the house."

"You're the expert, Doctor Howell, but would she have had time between when she arrived and died, for the poison to kill her?" the chief asked.

She looked across the soda shop, silent for over a minute. The chief was twitching in his chair, restless for an answer, and only slightly comforted when Horace held up a finger to let him know he should be patient. "Yes," Beatrix finally answered. "Some poisons are very fast acting. Digitalis takes time to be absorbed into the system, but considering the warmth of the room, the tension among the women elevating one's blood pressure, and the extra weight she was carrying, the answer is yes.

"Doctor Balfour, Doctor Theo Balfour, that is, and I found very generous traces on both of her cheeks, behind her right ear, on the back of her right hand, and ah, to be blunt, her décolletage," Beatrix said, blushing slightly.

"Back of her right hand?" the chief asked.

"Yes, a bit of blow-back from the squeeze bulb and spray. It would be similar to gunpowder residue on the gun hand of a shooter." She looked up and smiled.

"Digitalis, this poison that creates a heart attack, coming from a perfume atomizer that we can't find, that no one remembers, and you're the only one who saw it..." the chief said in frustration. "Look, I don't want to doubt you, but are you sure you saw it?"

Before Beatrix could answer Horace jumped in. "Chief, if Doctor Howell says she remembers seeing that atomizer, she saw the atomizer. It was there. It was on the vanity in the powder room. Find the atomizer and you have the murderer."

"There is something else that you both should know," Beatrix said quietly, leaning in toward them and lowering her voice. "During the funeral Mrs. Vandenberg whispered to me that she and some of the women are having a meeting tomorrow afternoon to talk over their plans for the garden tour. She wants me to be there."

"Looks like you're an insider now," Horace said.

"No, Horace. I do not have a single pot of petunias, so I am hardly a worthy member of their club. My belief is that the expressed purpose of the meeting is a smokescreen for something else. I believe they are worried about their safety, seeing as how two of their members have been murdered. I believe they want me present to tell them how to keep safe," she replied.

"Or to keep them safe," Horace said quietly. "I trust you'll bring your thirty-two year old friend to get a little leverage."

"Of course. Always in my handbag," she told him.

The chief snorted in derision. "I didn't hear that part, about your friend, that is. The solution answer is to call off the meeting, lock the doors, shutter the windows and stay home."

"Well, that won't be the answer they want to hear," Horace said. "Are you going, Beatrix?"

"Yes. I do not believe I have anything to tell them they do not already know, and I will be careful not to divulge anything we know. Perhaps there will be a clue. We can always hope," she answered.

"We can always hope," both Horace and the police chief answered in unison.

"What time is this pow-wow convening?" Horace asked.

"Two o'clock, with tea and light refreshments, although I doubt anyone will be in the mood to eat anything. Not after the last time."

"Who belongs to the truck?" Horace asked Fred late that afternoon.

"Oh, that there belongs to a fellow named Liam Williams. He's that gardener and handyman I was telling you about. Pulls weeds, splits wood, washes windows, mows lawns, and clears out the clinkers from the furnace if a fellow hasn't gotten around to doing that chore yet. Or can't get up and down the cellar steps. That sort of work, if you get my drift. Like I told you, he's a bit simple, but he's a steady worker and no doubt about it," Fred explained.

"Well, let's go meet my new employee. You don't happen to know how much I'm paying him, do you?" Horace asked.

"I sure do. Going rate around here is sixty-five cents an hour. See, the way I sort of looked at it was like this. You'd pay him the going rate on account of what's fair is fair. Fair to you, fair to him, and fair to the other folks that hire him, your neighbors and such-like. Course, at the end of the season, if you saw fit to slip him a few extra dollars, well, it would help see him through the winter a bit easier. Or, a little bonus if he does a good job during the week. You don't need to get too carried away on account of the fact you already gave him a two buck signing bonus."

"I did, did I?" Horace asked, half-amused.

"Yes, sir, General. I figured was the right thing to do, so I helped things along a bit."

"Good man, Sergeant. Liam, you say?" Horace asked as the two men walked across the lawn.

"Mr. Williams, I take it?" Horace asked, extending his hand.

"Yes, Sir, but everyone calls me Liam. It's a short version of my first name. William. People laughed at me when they heard I was called William William." He was busily trying to transfer some of the dirt and grime off his hands onto his cover-alls. "It's a real nice place you got here, and the garden ought to be looking nice real quick. Good soil. That's why the weeds are growing so well." He looked down at two piles at his feet, put his left foot behind his right leg, and tried to wipe the dirt off his shoe.

"Now, that's interesting. There's a pile of weed and a pile of dead flowers," Horace observed.

"Yes sir, there is that. I use the two pile system. Well, I sort of invented it. You see, the flowers go into an area sort of behind Miss Smith's flower shop. She let me dig a pit there, you see. That's where the flowers and leaves go after a while, and I mix in a little dirt and dried horse manure. I like it dried out or it gets too hot, you see, except late in the fall when I like the hot. That way it sort of cooks like a while longer. The manure and flowers sit there for a while and then I turn it over every once in a while so I can add it to a flower or vegetable bed, and they grow even better. I'm not the only one who does it. I read about it in the Old Farmer's."

"And the pile of weeds?" Horace asked.

"Oh, I take them out in the woods and dump 'em out and I'm done with them. Sooner or later Mother Nature will take its course and they'll rot away. But you see, these flowers, this time next year they'll be mixed in with the soil and you'll have even better ones. That's for sure," Liam said with pride.

"Perhaps we'll find out," Horace replied. "Carry on."

To his surprise, Horace was on his own that evening. Fred was away as a guest to the Elk's annual festival when they hosted the Odd Fellows for a "big feed" before they closed the lodge rooms for their summer holiday. Theo and Clarice were going to the Big Pavilion to watch an Al Jolson movie, and Beatrix was going to Ox-Bow with Phoebe and Harriet. As much as he liked his solitude, when it didn't come on his terms, he was restless and frustrated. "I'm stuck in the waiting room – again, thunderation!" he fumed. He paced the house for a few minutes, walked out to look at the freshly weeded garden, and plopped down hard on a side porch rocking chair.

Every few minutes, when there was little traffic and a whiff of wind from the right direction, Horace was convinced he could hear accordion music coming from a park. Out of sheer desperation to alleviate the boredom he decided to walk toward the music. He hoped it would be an interesting diversion.

He arrived at the little park near the river just in time to see Whistlin' Bill packing up his accordion. "Slow night?" Horace asked.

"You said it, brother. Sit yourself down on the bench. I welcome the company." He patted the bench seat. "Now, if you want a song or two, I'll be happy to get the old squeezebox out again," he offered.

Horace reached in his pocket. "Here's a bribe to leave that accordion in the case," Horace chuckled, handing him a two dollar bill.

"Much appreciated Doc, even if some folks are scared of a two dollar bill. So, how are you coming along on the murder? Solving it, I mean."

"As my folks would have said back in Minnesota, 'Not so good'. If you have some ideas I'm open to listening."

He tipped his head back and laughed. "You know, that's sort of funny. You see, most folks are more interested in talking than listening, especially when they can talk about themselves. And here you are, smart man like you, a genuine doctor and all, asking my advice. You know Doc, I appreciate it." He stuck out his right hand to shake Horace's hand.

"The way I look at it Doc, people have their own ideas about what's right and what's wrong. I've had people come up to me and say that I'm playing my accordion the wrong way. Now, I know they don't think I ought to turn it upside down and play the keys with my left hand and the buttons with my right. But what they mean is, I'm not playing a tune the right way. They'll think it is too fast or too slow, or I'm playing it in the wrong key. Or, they'll say that's not the way they heard it before. Maybe they're right or maybe they're wrong, but instead of just enjoying the music, maybe even dancing with their best girl or best guy, they're telling me what's wrong.

"People are like that about most things. Politics, for sure. Their party is always right and the other fellow, if he doesn't belong to the same party, is wrong. Always. It's been that way since Adams and Jefferson were around. You know why most people like Mr. Coolidge? It's because he doesn't say much. Silent Cal is probably the smartest man we ever had because he keeps his mouth shut, and it's hard to pick a fight with someone who doesn't fight back.

"Politics, religion – now there's a couple of big ones, or how a garden should be planted or a fishing hook baited. They'll go at it hammer and tong about it, and they get their backs up over it. Now, you know how everyone calls me 'Whistlin' Bill'? Well, there's a young lad here in town, Rollie's boy, and he likes to whistle, too. Now, if he was to ask me to teach him, I'd do it. Do it in a heartbeat, because he's got the gift. It's a genuine, for-real gift, I tell you. Some day he'll be famous around here for his whistling. You wait and see. But I'm not going to take him to task about how he does it because, well, he's having fun, enjoying himself. Why should I decide my way is better than his?

"So, you want my opinion, I'd say that whoever is the killer has had too many people telling him what he's done wrong for too long. And, if people keep doing that to him, it wouldn't surprise me if you've got another murder on your hands."

The two men sat in silence for a few minutes, then Horace said, "You've given me a lot to think over. Thank you."

"I ought to be thanking you. Most times everyone else does the talking and I do the listening."

FOURTEEN

LATE THE FOLLOWING AFTERNOON...

"Horace!" Beatrix shouted as she turned the doorbell key. "Horace! Are you here?"

He pulled open the front door. "Yes. I'm here. I was in my study. What's wrong, or what's new?"

"Yes," she said, "I can see that you are here. You are standing right in front of me. I have something I must tell you."

He stepped aside so she could come in his house, then trailed her to his study. "I believe that you might want to sit down," she told him.

"Mrs. Zimmerman is not Mrs. Zimmerman," she told him emphatically.

"Who is Mrs. Zimmerman."

"Horace, I just told you she is not Mrs. Zimmerman."

"Beatrix, let's try this again. Who is the woman I don't know, and why isn't Mrs. Zimmerman, Mrs. Zimmerman/"

"She is Mrs. Zuiderhoeff from Holland. That is her real name. And before you ask, the Holland that is in Michigan. It is just to the north of us."

"All right, I know that. Mrs. Zuiderhoeff is the woman we mistakenly thought was Mrs. Zimmerman, but how do I know her?"

"When we went down the basement stairs for Miss Stymington's funeral ...." She paused to look at him.

Horace smiled, "Now I remember her. One of the women down there who was giving Mrs. Vandenberg what for! Sure, I remember her now. All right, so why is this important?"

"Because she is also Mrs. Vandenberg's maid, and because her name isn't Zimmerman but Zuiderhoeff. Now do you understand? She works in the kitchen, maybe she is the chairwomen of the church kitchen ladies at the Church of the Heavenly Blessed, so she could have been in the kitchen waiting to kill Miss Stymington. She got into an argument with Mrs. Vandenberg, but she is also her maid. And, she is here under an assumed name!"

"Are you sure?" Horace asked, his mouth half open.

"Yes," Beatrix said calmly

"But how did you find out? Did you ask her?"

Beatrix smiled. "No, and I am not telling how I found out because it was not on the up and up. Do not ask. We never saw each other, Mrs. Zuiderhoff and me, that is. However, I could hear Mrs. Vandenberg and our Mrs. Zimmerman in the kitchen, and I recognized their voices. I must confess that I partially fibbed and said I needed to get something out of my car, and since I knew the cars that belonged to the other women, the other one had to belong to Mrs. Zimmerman. It was more road-worn than the others, so I assumed I might be right. I wrote down her license plate.

"My plan had been to leave as early as possible and drive to the police station to ask for the owner's name. As luck would have it, there really was a policeman when I needed him! I gave the number to the constable and he assured me he would take it forthwith to the chief and the chief would get back to me. I asked for the chief to come here. I trust you do not object too much to be making advantage of your hospitality."

Horace was silent and shook his head. "No. No, not at all. Of course not. I am delighted you did that because I want to hear what he has to say."

Beatrix looked at him and said, "And if I am right, then perhaps we have brought the murders to an end."

A few minutes later Chief Clarke knocked on the front door, and when Horace opened it, he had a big smile on his face. "I don't know how Doctor Howell did it, but she hit a home run like the Babe himself knocking it clear out of the ball park. I had to check twice to make sure it was right. Mrs. Zimmerman really is a Mrs. Zuiderhoeff."

Beatrix smiled and blushed at the compliment, then looked down.

"I drove past the place and dropped off one of my men to make sure she doesn't leave, then came right over here to tell you. I sort of figured you deserved to know. I'm going back over there and bring her in for questioning."

Beatrix gasped. "No, please slow down!"

"What's the matter?" the chief asked. "She looks pretty suspicious to me – phony name, arguing with the other women the way you said she was doing. I can't think of a single reason not to bring her in for questioning, can you?"

"Yes," Beatrix said. "I agree the situation does seem highly suspicious. It certainly did to me earlier this afternoon, and you have now verified it. But there may be a rational explanation for why she changed her name. And, people do argue and disagree all the time without committing murder."

"Sure, but...."

"If there is a good explanation, then why humiliate her in front of Mrs. Vandenberg? She will lose no opportunity to tell others. She will be blacklisted from their kitchens, the church, perhaps elsewhere. There is already too much pain in the world. We do not need to ruin her life, at least not yet."

"I sort of see your point, Doctor Howell. I hope you have a plan..."

Beatrix remained silent for a few minutes then said slowly and carefully, "Yes. I will go over to Mrs. Vandenberg's house with you, but in my car. I would be grateful if you park a distance away so you can watch the back door, and the officer who is there can remain on watch at the front of the house. I will go to the back door and ask her to come with me. We will walk to my car and return here."

"Here?" the chief asked. "Why?"

"Yes, here. If that is all right with you, Horace?" she asked.

"Of course," he said even though he was not following her line of reasoning. "It makes good sense. She is more likely to talk here than at the station house."

The chief reluctantly agreed. "You are putting yourself in danger. You realize that, don't you, Doctor Howell?"

"Yes. I believe, however, the danger is minimal."

"I didn't like Miss Stymington and I didn't care much for Mrs. Gray, and I sure as anything don't like Mrs. Vandenberg, either, except that she pays me to work for her. But that doesn't mean I killed any of them," Mrs Zuiderhoef said defiantly, when she was sitting nervously on the edge of a chair in Horace's office.

"I can see your point. There are plenty of folks I don't like, and I'm real glad that not everyone who dislikes me hasn't killed me, or even tried. You have a good point there," the chief said, nodding in agreement. When she started to relax, the chief smiled at her. "But I am trying to figure out who did it, and you can help. Maybe you're the only who can help. To start off, it seems your real name is Zelda Zuiderhoef, but you go by Zimmerman. Right now, that raises my eyebrows, all things considered, just now. I guess you can figure out why" He looked at her and said nothing, waiting for her to answer.

Very quietly, her head down, she said, "It is a story that brings me shame. When I was in elementary school we lived on a farm outside of Dorr, and this one day we had a substitute teacher. She did the roll call, using our last name and first initial: Zuiderhoef – Z. Well, Pa was a drunkard, and one of the boys kept saying, 'Zuiderzee, her father drinks like a fish in the sea.' They'd tease me all the time with it until I cried. I left school at the end of the eighth grade, mostly to get away, moved to Holland, and got a job cleaning at the hotel out on Lake Macatawa, and I changed my name and never looked back."

"You had a rough time," Beatrix said quietly. "So much pain."

"You don't know the half of it," Mrs. Zimmerman sobbed.

The chief was slow to speak. "Well, changing your name like that, that's certainly understandable. Look, help us with the next part, and then no one will have to know your private business, leastwise not from us. Look, you were heard having an argument in the church kitchen..."

"Yes. If that busy-body hadn't been lording it over me, over us...." Mrs. Zimmerman spat out angrily.

"I understand. But you also have the keys to the church, and since you run the kitchen, and since Miss Stymington was found in the kitchen.... Well, you see how it looks, don't you?"

"I come down there and clean up the church kitchen real early on Mondays. This time of year, right around sunrise. I want to get in there, do my work, and get out before the secretary or the minister or anyone else comes in and tries telling me how to do my business. I didn't see Miss Stymington that day. I try, well, tried, to avoid her as much as possible."

"So, no one saw you come in, do the cleaning, and then leave?" Horace asked.

"You got that one right," Mrs. Zimmerman said, almost defiantly. "I like it that way."

"You realize that you have no alibi, then?" Horace asked.

"That's not my fault, now is it? Anyways, honest folk don't need to come up with alibis all the time, now do they? I got there around 5:30 or so, cleaned up after the coffee hour on Sunday. You know, washed and dried the dishes and cups and put them away. After that, I cleaned off the counters and swept the floor. After that I hung up my apron and the towels and went home."

"About what time?" the chief asked.

"Around 7:30 or so. It usually takes me a couple of hours to get everything looking the way I want it to."

"Mrs. Zimmerman, did you see a display of flowers in the kitchen?" Beatrix asked.

She looked at her, puzzled, and answered, "I don't remember. I get paid to keep the kitchen clean and tidy, not look at poesies. So, I don't know. I keep the kitchen clean because that's the way I like it, and when we have a church *do*, I run a tight ship."

The chief blew the air of his cheeks in frustration. He slowly stood up, stretched, and motioned Horace and Beatrix to follow him into the front parlor. "By rights, I ought to hold her on suspicion of murder," the chief said softly.

"But you do not want to do that, do you?" Beatrix asked, hoping she would hear the right answer.

"Seems a bit harsh to me," Horace answered, solemnly nodding in agreement.

"Would you allow me to talk privately with her for a few moments? She may be more open if it is woman to woman," Beatrix suggested.

"I can't figure that woman out," the chief said to Horace as they sat in the parlor. "Doc Howell, not the other woman. One moment she is icy…"

Horace interrupted him. "Detached is the right word. A good forensic pathologist has to be detached."

"Detached, then. Then she turns around and can tell when someone is in pain. I don't get her. I just don't get her."

Horace pulled out his pipe and lit it. "Welcome to a very large club. I can't either, and I've probably known her as long, if not longer than anyone. My guess is she's had her share, and more, of pain, but she's never mentioned it. That's why when she sees someone else… well, like you said…. Anyway, she's probably the most brilliant pathologist I've ever met, and has an absolute encyclopedic mind. If she reads or sees something, she remembers it. Never forgets a thing. I admire and appreciate her brainpower."

"I heard she flies a plane? Is that true?" the chief asked.

"It is. I've been in it a few times. Fortunately, she's got it stored at a hangar in Holland. And, she's got a Detroit Electric for around town, and turns right around and owns a snappy little Marmot for the road. Not that she ever goes very far, mind you. She's written ground-breaking medical papers but freezes up speaking in front of a crowd, so she won't do it. And when she retired from full time practice, she took all that brain power and became a renowned art forensic pathologist. Eccentric enough for you? It's just the beginning."

"So, how did she end up in Saugatuck?" the chief asked.

"One word, well, a hyphenated one, 'Ox-Bow'. Dr. Howell learned about the place and came here to take up oil painting. I re-met her through my daughter-in-law. She's like all retired physicians – wants to keep her hands in the profession a bit and as far as I'm concerned, Saugatuck is fortunate to have a pathologist like her."

The chief interrupted. "You want to know something? I think I'm the lucky one she's here. Without her, we'd never have realized those two society dames were murdered."

"Don't get ahead of yourself. Right now, we'll be lucky if we figure out who killed them."

They turned toward the study door when they heard Beatrix opening it.

"All right, Mrs. Zimmerman, I could hold you for further questioning, but you can thank Doctor Howell for a little compromise. I'll let you leave, but I want your promise that you will call my office every morning at eight, and then again at six in the evening. I want your solemn word that you'll do that, or else I'll think you've run off, and that is a serious offense. You can work, shop, do whatever it is you do, as long as you don't leave the area and you call me twice a day. Do we have a deal?" the chief asked.

She nodded her head and barely murmured "Thank you."

"Well, you can go. I'm sure I'm going to need your help in the near future."

Mrs. Zimmerman turned to Beatrix, "Thank you. You're a good one. You're not like those other hoity-toity women."

"You are welcome," Beatrix said. "By the way, I am always curious about names and places. Zimmerman is German, is it not?"

"No, Doctor Howell, Swiss. My folks, they came from a German canton in Switzerland."

"I understand. Thank you," Beatrix said.

"What was that about – asking about Zimmerman being German?" Horace asked.

Beatrix smiled. "Curiosity." She turned to the chief. "I would encourage you to talk with Bobby at the telephone office, and ask her to make sure that when Mrs. Zimmerman calls it is from her home in Holland."

"You think she might skip out on us?" the chief asked.

"One never knows," she smiled.

MURDER OF THE SAUGATUCK CHURCH BASEMENT KITCHEN LADIES

FIFTEEN

Chief Clarke stood in the doorway of Horace's office for a few seconds, not wanting to interrupt him, but finally coughed and knocked softly on the wooden frame. "Hate to interrupt you, Doc, but I got a strange one."

"A strange one, of what sort?" Horace asked.

The chief winced. "Well, it's like this. I just got a call from Mickey Smith, you know, the flower shop lady. She'd closed up for a few minutes to go to the bank, and when she got back to her shop there was an envelope in the door with five saw-bucks in it and...."

"Let me take a guess, an order for a Bird of Paradise to be delivered, and no name on the note," Horace said.

"I guess that wasn't so hard to figure out. Well, she called me and I'm just about to run over there. You and maybe Doctor Howell want to come along with me?"

"I'll go, but right now Doctor Howell and my brother are looking at some tissue samples and trying a new technique to get them to show up better under a microscope. I don't think they can be interrupted. Well, they could be interrupted, but I doubt they'd like it. " He looked at his watch, then said, "They're likely going to be tied up until at early afternoon. Knowing Beatrix, she'll work through lunch if she has to.. Let me tell the secretary I'm stepping out for a few minutes."

"Here's the envelope and the note and the money," Miss Smith said, showing them to the chief and Horace.

"And you say you found it in the door?" the chief asked.

"Between the screen door and glass one, right where I'd see it when I walked in," she said.

"Now, please think carefully. Has anyone else touched any of this paper? Anyone at all?" Horace asked.

"No, I doubt it. I wasn't gone that long, just to the bank and back, and I'm the only one here. So, no, probably not, but I won't swear on the Good Book about it because I might be mistaken," she said. "I didn't do anything wrong, did I?"

Chief Andrew smiled. "No. You certainly didn't. You did the right thing calling me. Thanks to your quick thinking, we may get a clue that solves these murders." He used his penknife to open the letter so he could read it aloud. "'Bird of Paradise to Josephine Trimble in Shorewood'". He looked up at her and asked, "Miss Smith, is she a regular customer of yours?"

"Who? You mean Miss Trimble? She buys flowers when she's having a dinner party or special occasions. She wasn't a big spender, just like the others."

"Others...what" Horace asked.

"You know, the others in the Garden Tea Club," Miss Smith answered. "She made up for being a tight-wad by being more demanding, you know, giving orders and acting like I was supposed to jump-to."

"So, when are you supposed to deliver this flower?" the chief asked.

"I'll have to make a long distance call to the wholesaler in Chicago and then they send it up on the train the next day. That is, if they got 'em."

The chief was silent for a moment or two, thinking. "Okay, I know it's still early in the day and you might lose some business. I'd like you to close up for the day and go home. If you don't mind, I'd like you to stay there until we get back from this Mrs. Trimble's place and we'll either call you or stop by."

Miss Smith shrugged her shoulders. "I'll just put a note on the door..."

"Hold on a moment," Horace said. "We don't know who is sending these letters and we don't know what they're up to. There is a possibility, just a slight one, you might be in danger. You're safer going home, locking the doors, and staying there, at least until we get back. There is a chance they might not know where you live. Just put a note that you're out on a call."

"I think he's right," the chief added. "Besides, I haven't got enough men to keep an eye on the shop and on your place."

Miss Smith tightened her lips and muttered something under her breath about a lot of fuss. "You mind if I lock up my work room?" She didn't wait for an answer, got up, and locked it. When the three of them stepped outside, she locked the front door.

"If things look like they're on the up and up, I'll shoot right over to your place and let you know. Then, it's up to you if you want to open up again," the chief told her.

"Let me know either way, would you?" she insisted.

"You sure this is the right place?" Horace asked Chief Andrew.

"Well, there's the Red Chapel and we're on Lakeshore Road, and this is the house two doors down from the church. It's got to be the right place," he answered, trying the front door, then knocking loudly on the window. "Maybe she's not home."

"I'll go see if the neighbors might know something," Horace said, "while you look around in back." Ten minutes later Horace returned. "Nothing. The neighbor lady said that Mrs. Trimble usually went to the beach most afternoons, but she hadn't gone today. Far as she knows, at least."

"Yeah, and her car is around in back," the chief said, walking over to the front window. He cupped his hand and looked inside. He let out a low whistle. "This doesn't look good."

"What is it?"

"I can't rightly see, but it looks like someone's stretched out on the couch." He pounded on the window, paused, and then louder. They could hear a dog inside, but whoever was on the couch didn't move. "I don't think she's having a snooze, not with that yappy dog making all that noise. Let's go around in back and see what that door is like. Maybe we'll get lucky and it won't be locked."

Luck was not with them, and Chief Andrew put his shoulder to the door, rammed it twice, and the door opened.

"Definitely deceased," Horace said after trying to find a pulse. He stood back, next to the chief, so they could look at the body on the couch. She was on her right side, her left arm dropped to the floor, and an empty glass had rolled out of her hand and onto the floor about a foot away.

"What do you think?" the chief asked. "Natural causes or suicide?"

"No idea, and if there is one thing I've learned from Doctor Howell, it is never to rush into a diagnosis. Better call for an ambulance and get her to the hospital. And then call the hospital and tell her its bag and gown time."

"You want her to come out here?"

"Not nearly as much as you *will* want her here. We'd better not touch a thing until she takes a look at it. If we're lucky they've wrapped things up and Theo will be here, too."

"What about their science research?" the chief asked.

"This takes priority. And Chief, you might tell her where we are. It would help if she knows where to go."

"It appears very straight forward," Beatrix said bleakly after she completed her examination. "The subject died of a massive heart attack and the glass next to her contained almost pure digitalis." She looked at Horace, the chief, and Theo, then cocked her head. "The smell is very strong."

"In other words, suicide," Chief Andrew asked.

"Not necessarily, and please do not jump to conclusions. I only know she died of a heart attack induced by consuming a significant amount of digitalis. Only the circumstantial evidence clearly indicates she chose to take her own life. Anything beyond that can lead us into dangerous speculation."

Horace ignored her advice.

"Well, that looks like the explanation and end of the murders. Two homicides and a suicide," Horace told the chief, Beatrix, and his brother Theo. "For whatever reason, she killed two people and then took her own life."

"That's that, then," Theo added quietly. "It's terribly sad isn't it? I suppose we'll never learn the reason why she killed two friends. Pure madness."

"I'll be looking into that part until I get a satisfactory answer," the chief said quietly but firmly.

Beatrix was surprisingly angry. "I did not say it was suicide or homicide. You heard me! I said we had evidence only that she died of digitalis poisoning, and even that is mere speculation." She stamped her foot in frustration. "Why must you be so quick to jump to conclusions. Horace and Theo, you know better than that. And chief, you *should* know better!"

They watched as Beatrix walked out of the room to the porch, standing still, her left hand reaching across her front to hold her right arm.. Horace knew she was reviewing every object she had seen in the room, fixing the images in her mind, and trying to make the connections. A few minutes later, out of her surgical gown and gloves, she walked past the window.

"Any idea where Fred is?" Theo asked.

"No, why?" his brother answered.

"I was thinking it might be nice if he'd see if Beatrix wants a lift to the airport in Holland. She'd probably feel better if she went up in her plane," Theo replied.

"Well, she would probably enjoy the drive alone," Horace told him.

"You know, big brother, there are times when I really wonder if you have a heart. The woman is hurting, and the offer is what counts, whether she takes him up on it or not," Theo said in disgust.

Horace thought over his brother's comments for a few moments, then silently walked out to the front porch to join her.

"You don't have to do this," Beatrix told him.

"I know," he said quietly. "Thunderation! Sometimes I just seem to have this urge to get away from here for a little while right now, especially when I acted like a first year medical student and rushed ahead. I just thought.... Well, I used to have a boat to make a get-away." He smiled thinly.

"Even in an aeroplane? You're terrified of it," she said warily.

"I know that, too. Maybe I should have kept the boat. Let's go," he said quietly, nodding toward his car.

Beatrix opened the door and got in the front seat. "To the hospital. We have an autopsy first." She rode in silence until they arrived at the hospital. She turned and said distantly, "You are a good man, a friend."

Church Kitchen Ladies Sixteen

Theo eventually joined his brother and Beatrix, but too late to gown for the autopsy. He perched on a tall wheeled exam stool, staying out of their way.

The autopsy had been relatively fast. Just as Horace, Theo, and Beatrix suspected, Mrs. Trimble had died of a heart attack brought on by the digitalis. "Listen, why don't you two take off and Dr. Landis and I can close up," Theo offered. He looked at his brother to make sure he understood the implication. He did.

"Don't forget to let the chief know the results," Horace said. He looked at his pocket watch. "Doesn't seem like there is much sense in Miss Smith opening her shop again, does it?"

It was about an hour and a half before sunset when they pushed Beatrix's bi-plane out of the hangar onto the grass runway at the Holland airfield. She did the pre-flight checks and smiled. "I know, front seat," Horace told her.

"Good. I like a man who can learn fast. Do not forget your helmet and goggles. I will check to make sure you are buckled in. It is not that I do not trust you, but, well, I want to be sure."

They flew over Lake Macatawa, listening to the engine of her plane until she was satisfied all was well. Beatrix pulled back on the stick to gain altitude as they flew over Big Red Lighthouse. She banked and flew south along the shore until they came to the breakwater at the mouth of the Kalamazoo River and turned inland. They were approaching the old city water pump house when Beatrix dived sharply. Horace turned back to look at her, and saw her point down toward the river. "Look familiar?" she shouted at him.

He was beaming and shook his head in agreement. It was his old boat, the *Aurora*, now Captain and Mrs. Garwood's sightseeing boat. Considerable work and expense had gone into the old paddle wheeler, and that summer it instantly became one of the village's tour destinations. Beatrix dropped the plane down low, levelled off, and suddenly pulled up a hundred yards from the vessel, banked, as both she and Horace waved to the captain. He answered with several loud blasts on the whistle.

She levelled off and followed the Kalamazoo upriver to New Richmond, using the railroad trestle as a landmark, and began the return to Holland. Horace turned around to look at her, cheered to see that she had a broad smile on her face. At least for a few minutes, she felt free. As he turned forward again he happened to spot something below that caught his interest. With his index finger pointing up, he made a broad sweep of his left hand, then pointed down.

She circled, and with him looked over the left side of the plane to the ground below. "See it!" she shouted. "Down." Beatrix banked again, made a long circle, then switched off the engine to glide silently over the small building below. Once they had passed over it, she started the engine again and they quickly gained altitude and returned immediately to the airfield in Holland.

As soon as the plane had taxied to a stop, both of them pulled off their leather helmets. "This isn't over!" Horace shouted, forgetting he was no longer trying to be heard over the engine. "I do not think Mrs. Trimble is the murderer or committed suicide!" Beatrix told him loudly, still partially deafened from the roar of the plane's motor. "You are right. This is not over!"

"We need to call the chief, tell him to say and do nothing, and have him meet us at my home," Horace said. They hurriedly pushed Beatrix's plane into the hanger, turned it around to face out, and then called Chief Andrew from the control shack.

"I'll drive," Beatrix said.

"It's my car," Horace retorted.

"Yes, but you do not know how to make good use of an accelerator. Sometimes you drive like an old lady," she told him.

"Thunderation woman! I wouldn't bring age into this discussion if I were you. There's no reason to break our necks for a couple of extra minutes." Horace hurriedly got behind the steering wheel before Beatrix beat him to it.

"What in the world is going on?" the chief demanded when Horace and Beatrix hurried up the front walked of his house and found him waiting on the front porch swing.

"Beatrix and I were up in her plane...." Horace started.

"I find it refreshing and sometimes I do my best thinking when I am up by about a thousand feet," a very composed Beatrix interrupted to explain. "Go ahead, Horace."

"We flew up the Kalamazoo River to New Richmond and back, and on the return we followed the Old Allegan Road, about a mile or so from the railroad bridge, we looked down and..."

"Boss, I sure am glad to see you. Me and Miss Phoebe went out for a driving lesson down along Old Allegan Road, and you'd never believe what we done did see when we were there," Fred said loudly as he came up the front walk. "Say, Doc, did I hear you up in your plane?"

"Would one of you mind starting and finishing your story, please? I'm falling behind," the chief said.

"Just off to the right a mile or so this side of the railroad bridge, there's a road. Now, a few hundred yards back there's a thicket of trees and a clearing. You can't see it from the road. From the air, we could see it clear as anything, and I think there's something fishy going on there," Horace said.

"See what? Chief Andrew asked. "What makes you think something's fishy?

Horace paused, searching for words, giving Fred a chance to join in. "A shack, Chief. A little shack."

"Real simple, Chief, Phoebe and I were out along that there road, and we saw Mickey Smith the flower lady pull onto that side road. I told Phoebs not to wave, not to look, but to keep going fast like we were in a hurry to get somewheres, and she done did just that. We went down the road a ways until we came to another driveway and turned around, and then parked the car to the side of Old Allegan and we crept through the bushes like I did when I heard a bunch of Hun soldiers up ahead of me in the spring of 1918.

"And sure enough, we saw that there Miss Smith hand the gardener fellow who works for folks, a big box of dead flowers..." Fred explained.

"All right, that is a bit odd, but I don't think there is anything illegal about it," the chief said.

"Well, let me tell you, you wouldn't be saying that if you knew what type of flowers she gave him – foxglove. A lot of foxglove," Fred said. "of the poisonous variety. She done did give him those flowers and then took off out of there again."

"All right," the chief answered as he began to make the connections.

"Chief, foxglove is the common name of digitalis. She was giving him the basic ingredient for making the poison that has killed three people," Beatrix explained slowly and carefully.

"Don't you mean the flowers that killed two and the other a suicide?" the chief asked.

"I am not so sure anymore. There is a good reason to believe that all three were homicides," Horace told him. Beatrix nodded in agreement.

"That's pretty thin evidence to even question this fellow. Liam, Liam William, that's his name, isn't it?" the chief asked.

"There may be a little more to the story," Fred added. "Like I was saying, me and Phoebe pulled over to the side of the road and went through the bushes until we sneaked around so we could get a good look into that there shed. I told her to stay put and be quiet while I slipped in a little closer, and I got a good look at what he was up to.

"He had a ringer washer set up in there, sort of fixed up so it caught the juice on the far end, and he was running those foxglove plants through the rollers. Good thing he had one of those little Popping Johnnies so he couldn't hear me coming. I can't say that there was a lot of juice coming out of it, but it was a pretty steady trickle. All I know is that you have to be shell shocked or tetched in the head to spend an afternoon squeezing dead plants if you aren't up to something you shouldn't be up to doing. Maybe he's our man!"

Chief Andrews sat silently, taking it all in and trying to make sense of it. "That doesn't sound good," he finally said. "I've seen the fellow around and he seems quiet and harmless enough. Doesn't talk much but I hear he's a steady worker. He sure doesn't mix in much. Sort of simple, that's what people say about him, if you get my drift. You never think of someone like that being a cold blooded killer."

"Perhaps he is not," Beatrix said quietly.

The chief ignored her. "Well, I've got to have a talk with that fellow, and I hope for his sake he's got a good explanation for what he's doing. You know, that fellow would have access into almost any place in town. Working out in back like that, on his own, and most folks never locking their doors," the chief said.

"The sort of person who is there, but you don't really see," Horace added. He looked at Beatrix and added, "Well, the sort of person most of us don't see."

"We had a couple of boys like that in our platoon right when I joined up. Didn't have any stripes yet, being new and all. Real quiet-like and didn't mix in. Never knew what they were thinking. None of us wanted to buddy up with 'em when we went out on a patrol. One corporal said fellows like that are as likely to shoot you in the back as they were the Hun. There might be something to that, you know. Maybe this Liam fellow is that way."

"I'll get a couple of the boys and go have a look around," the chief said as he stood up. "Fred, you mind riding shotgun with me so you can show me where this place is since you said it's hidden."

"You wait right here and I'll go get my bird gun," Fred smiled.

"Fred, I believe the police chief was using a figure of speech, asking you to sit in the passenger's seat of his automobile," Beatrix carefully explained.

"Yeah, I sort of had an idea what he meant, but you can't blame an old soldier for trying," he said grinning at her. "Makes me feel better to have something that shoots back if it comes to that."

"Let's go down to the station and get a couple of the fellows, and we'll go out there," the chief said. "You folks might want to stay right around here until we get back."

"If it's all the same to you, I think we'd like to come along," Horace said.

"I agree with Doctor Balfour," Beatrix said firmly.

"Suit yourselves, but you've put in a long day, remember," the chief told them.

Liam's old truck was still at the shack. There was no sign of Miss Smith's vehicle. As they neared the building chief and an officer, Horace, Beatrix, Fred, and Phoebe could hear the sound of a small gas engine turning the rollers. "Still at it," the chief said.

"Let us hope so," Beatrix whispered back.

They moved closer, keeping quiet, the two police officers with their pistols drawn. Either Liam didn't hear them, or was concentrating on his work, but suddenly he heard Chief Andrew shout, "Hands up, Williams, and turn around slowly." The gardener's eyes widened in fear when he saw the pistols aimed at his chest.

"Fred, turn off that engine, would you?" the chief asked. He turned back to Liam and said, "You've got a little explaining to do. What's going on here? What are you up to? Who are you working for?"

Williams was so rattled, without thinking he blurted out, "Mrs. Smith told me I wasn't suppose to say who I was working for, and besides, I'm not doing anything wrong. I'm just running these plants through the squeezer to get the juice out."

"Yeah, and then what? And where'd you get all these flowers? Who gave them to you?"

Liam doubled up in pain, folding his arms around his head. He was shaking. "So many questions. You're all talking at once and getting me mixed up. Stop it! I can't think with all of you talking at the same time. Stop it! Stop it! I haven't done nothing! You're scaring me!"

Beatrix's eyes widened, and she pushed past the constables to go to Liam Williams. "Please, put your pistols away. It is all right." The two patrolmen and the chief ignored her request.

She slowly walked toward the young men. "Mr. Williams. I am a doctor and here to help you. Will you let me help?" She awkwardly comforted him, taking his two hands in hers. "Mr. Williams, will it be all right if I ask everyone else to leave your building? Then you and I can talk quietly. If you want, Doctor Balfour can stay with us. You know him because you work for him. I think he is a good man. Do you agree with me that he is a good and kind doctor? And I believe you know Fred, too, do you not?"

Williams nodded he wanted the others to leave.

"Would you be more comfortable if you and I talked by ourselves?" She asked. When he nodded a second time Beatrix looked at Fred and indicated he should join the others outside. "Horace, come and let's talk with Mr. Williams, please."

Chief Andrews wasn't certain it was the right thing to do, and reluctantly holstered his pistol. He nodded to the constables to do the same. "Okay, boys, let's move back a bit. Doctor Howell, I think we'll go outside for some fresh air..." the chief said.

"What the devil is going on with that fellow?" the chief demanded after they left the little shack. He nervously watched the door.

"If you were to ask me, that fellow's got something like shell shock. I seen men without a scratch on them, just like that," Fred said.

"He's too young to have been in the war," the chief objected.

"You're right, but I didn't say he had shell shock, just something like it. He's hurting something bad, and he's scared. We just give

Doc Howell and the boss all the time they needs and you'll have all the intelligence you needs. You can bank on that."

They waited, and suddenly Fred started sniffing the air, then smiled. "That's a good sign, for sure, chief. You smell that? It's the boss and he's got his pipe lit. Everything's gonna be just fine now."

"Is that some sort of a signal?" the chief asked, then laughed, "You know, some sort of smoke signal?"

"Nah, well maybe. If he's really intense and focused on something, like when he's doing surgery and up to his elbow's in someone gut, he is all business. But when he relaxes and he's turning things over in his mind, then he pulls out his pipe, see? And that's what he's done did now."

"I hope you're right," the chief said, still watching the door.

SEVENTEEN

Horace and Beatrix came out of the shack, steadying Liam Williams between them. "Shell shock," Fred whispered. "I done did see it over there in France. Shell shock or something like it."

"I see what you mean," the chief said, still convinced that the man was far too young to have been in the war.

"I think Mr. Williams needs to sit down. Perhaps in the back seat of your police car, chief?" Horace asked. They helped him into the car, closed the door, and moved away so they could talk.

"We got our man!" the chief said in triumph.

"He is not our killer," Beatrix said quietly. "You heard him mention Mrs. Smith, and I believe he meant the florist in town."

"So, what's his line? How's he tied up with her?" the chief asked.

"Williams said that she pays him to take the flowers and separate them by type – roses, iris, and so on," Horace answered.

"And foxglove," Beatrix added.

"Right. And he crushes them to extract the juice and puts it into half-pint jars," Horace explained. "She told him she was trying to make perfume."

"Perfume my eye. He's making poison!" the chief snapped.

"Very likely that is what is happening, only he thinks he is helping her make new brands of perfume. That is what she told him, and he believes it," Horace said, pulling out his pipe.

"I believe that is exactly what he believes," Beatrix agreed. "We all know that he is a loner and very odd at times, and I think he may be a bit simple. He is easily impressionable. He is lonely and she apparently took pity on him."

"Or, took advantage of him and his condition," Horace said. "I don't know if she is trying to be the next Coco Chanel or not. But, I do believe Williams is telling the truth, We also need to open to the real possibility that Mrs. Smith doesn't understand what she is doing. It may be accidental or negligent homicide."

They stood silently, looking at each other.

"Well, let's take Williams down to the station house and make him comfortable in one of the cells. He'll be safe there. And then let's go have a talk with the Flower Fairy and see what she has to say about our Mr. Williams," the chief said slowly.

"I think that's a good idea," Horace agreed. "She might help us figure him out."

"May I suggest that you leave your constable there to keep close watch on him. He is quiet now, but later he may put himself in danger if he becomes agitated or frightened," Beatrix said. "I would advise you to leave the car with the constable in case he needs to be transported to the hospital in Holland."

"That seems like a real good idea," the chief said.

They left Williams in one of the cells. "Now look, we're not locking you in. We're going to close the door for your privacy, but that's it. We're not locking it. You're not under arrest or anything, but right now, this is the safest place in the world for you to be. Do you understand, Williams?"

The man nodded but said nothing.

"Now, please drive me to my house and I will get my car and follow behind you," Beatrix said.

"Why?" Horace asked.

"Because that is where I have my medical bag, should we need it," she said firmly.

"That makes good sense," the chief said.

When they arrived at the flower shop they discovered the door was still locked. "Sergeant, front and center!" Horace said loudly.

Fred flashed a big smile as he reached for his package of lock-picking tools. "That's not exactly legal," the chief objected.

"Funny, we hear that from time to time, don't, Sergeant?" Horace asked.

"Yes, sir, General. We sure do. A door is locked, someone wants to get in, and I help them and then they turn around and say it's not legal. That doesn't seem right to me." Fred winked at the chief to let him know he was teasing. He worked the rake and then the pick until he heard a satisfying snap. After he opened the door he bowed deeply and waved his arm so the chief could enter.

"Well done, Fred, Beatrix smiled as she entered. "As always."

For the next few minutes Chief Andrews, Fred, Horace and Beatrix, carefully looked around the flower shop. "Nothing seems out of order, outside of it being extremely untidy," Beatrix told them.

"Nothing but that back door. Now, that's strange. Mrs. Smith has got a padlock on the front door so people won't break in, but inside she's got that big dead-bolt on a door. That doesn't add up," the chief said. "I shouldn't ask this, but Fred...."

"I don't know about that one. I've opened a lot of locks before, but that one's new to me. I can try, but...." He knelt down to study the lock. "Two different keys, and I'll have to figure out which one to do first, or maybe both have to be turned at the same time. If that there is the case, I'm short one set of tools." He started working on it. He was muttering something under his breath.

After a few minutes the chief became impatient. "All right, let's flush her out. I told her to go home and stay there, and let's hope she is. He picked up the telephone and said, "Bobbie, would you put me through to Mickey Smith's home?"

When she answered, the chief told her that there was a possible break-in at her flower show, and wanted her to come right away. She agreed.

"Well, everything looks like it did when I left. What makes you think there was a break-in?" she asked when she arrived at her shop about fifteen minutes later.

"One of my fellows was doing a door check. You know, a couple of places, like the breakfast and lunch diners, close up early, so we check to make sure the doors are locked. Then we check them later at night to make sure they've stayed locked. I told him to make a point of checking your place. I guess the padlock was open on your front door. That's why I called you to come down," he explained casually.

"Oh, I must have been in a hurry and forgot! Thank you. It's been such a horrible day...." she answered anxiously.

The chief gave her a big smile. "Say, I'm kind of curious. You got that heavy duty lock on the closet door, and a pretty flimsy one on the front. I'm not exactly telling you what to do, but you might want to switch them around. What do you keep in there that's so valuable? Say, as long as we're here, we ought to make a thorough inspection to be sure you weren't burgled."

"That's really not necessary," she sputtered.

"Yeah. It really is. I assume you have the key either in your handbag or on the premises. Please open the door." The chief's voice was firm. It wasn't a request, but a command, and the smile disappeared from his face.

"Well, I keep the key in the little closet behind me. That's my storage and work room," she said.

"The key, please. Now." His voice was firm.

Mickey Smith turned to open the closet door and pulled a large key and ring off the nail. She handed it to the chief, and in a flash she turned around to take something out of the closet.

"I told you that was my workroom," Mrs. Smith said.

"Horace, that is a shotgun she is holding," Beatrix whispered hoarsely.

"I noticed that. A double barreled breach-loading sawed off shut gun," he answered calmly. Very short. The kick-back will probably knock her off her feet. Lethal, though, at close range."

"Horace! Thunderation! Do you realize every time we find the killer we end up having a gun pointed at us! You promised it would be different! You promised they would not get the jump on us!

"Sorry about that. I wasn't expecting that to happen."

"Well, you should have thought of it. O'Banion was a florist and a cold blooded mobster, too, you know."

Phoebe had returned home, just as her mother pulled into the driveway. "Did you have a nice day, dear?" Harriet asked as they walked into the house together.

"Yes! It was wonderful. Fred took me driving and we found the killer in a shack, and now Grandfather and Fred and Doctor Howell are with the police chief at Mrs. Smith's flower shop. Aren't you curious? We should go there." Phoebe asked.

"Oh, just a nice quiet routine day with your grandfather and Doctor Howell," she said sarcastically. "That sounds like a tall tale to me."

"We should drive over to the flower shop," Phoebe repeated, this time with greater urgency.

At first Harriet rejected the idea of driving to the shop to have a look, and then she said, "You know, maybe we should go. None of them really know the woman. Maybe we should, well, be there. To help, you know."

Phoebe smiled. Her mother's excuse was flimsy, but she knew her mother was as curious as she was.

The door to the shop was closed, but through the side window they could see that everything was very wrong. "It looks like a stick up!" Harriet whispered to her daughter.

"It's not a stick up. Grandpa let someone get the drop on them again. He's lets it happen every time."

"We should call the police," Harriet said.

"Mother, the police chief is in there. She got the drop on him, too.

Harriet drew in her breath in alarm. "What should we do? We've got to do something."

"And fast," her daughter whispered back.

Phoebe looked around and spotted Beatrix' car about half way down and across the street. "She's going to really be mad at me," she said to herself. "Mother I'll be right back, and when you see me, throw a rock or a brick or something through the window and yell 'bomb' at the top of your voice."

"What are you doing, young lady?" Harriet demanded, her eyes widening. Phoebe was already jogging down the street and slipped into Beatrix' car. It took her a few seconds to find everything on the dash board and remember how to make the car work. "Okay, this switch says "B". Battery! Power switch! Now where is the gas,I mean, electric pedal to make it go faster?" she talked to herself. She found a long lever on the floor that looked like it might work, and pushed it slightly. The car inched forward.

Phoebe swallowed hard and carefully got the car out on to the street. It was one thing to drive it the other day when she wasn't saving her grandfather. This time it was different. Her mouth was dry and she wasn't certain what to do. She put it into reverse to back up twenty some yards, brought the throttle to neutral, and then pushed it all the way forward. The electric car practically leapt down the street. She was frightened, but it was the response from the old car that she wanted. She took a deep breath.

Phoebe brought it to a stop, backed up, again. For a moment she rehearsed in her mind exactly what she would do. Back up, start up the street, full speed ahead, turn into the drive way, jump into the tall grass, roll, and hope for the best that she didn't break her neck. She swallowed hard, checked the street to make sure no one was on it or the sidewalk.

"Phoebe to the rescue. Here goes nothing!"

She raced down the street, turning left so sharply into the long driveway the car was on its right wheels, then collapsed back on all four again, just as she leapt out, rolling across the lawn.

Her mother watched in horror and yet remembered to throw the brick through the window of the shop and yelled "Bomb" a mere second before the Detroit Electric hit the building.

It was the distraction Horace and his companions needed. Mickey Smith turned to see what was happening behind her, giving the chief the opportunity to grab the barrel of the shotgun and turn it away from everyone and himself. They tussled for a second or two, giving Beatrix the opportunity to leap forward, cock her right arm, and smash her fist into Mrs. Smith's jaw. Beatrix let out a loud yelp of pain and had her right hand under her left arm. It was cold comfort to watch the florist slump to the floor.

And then it was over. Chief Andrew ejected the two shells from the shot gun, and Fred and Horace lifted Mrs. Smith off the floor and slapped her face until she came too. Beatrix, uncharacteristically for her, was hopping around the flower shop, holding her wrist in agony.

"I think it's broken, Horace," she said. Her face was white with pain.

"You might be right. Sprained at the very least. Next time you're going to try knocking someone out, remember to keep your wrist stiff."

"I can show you how to do it," Fred offered.

"Thank you, Horace, you always seem to know the right thing to say. You are such a comfort," Beatrix answered sarcastically. "What was that explosion? The whole building shook. Who threw the bomb?"

Phoebe and Harried charged through the front door, and the girl walked to where Beatrix was sitting. "Doctor Howell, we did. Only it wasn't a normal bomb. You're going to be really mad at me; I just know it. I'll pay for it. I promise I will. I really will. Mother threw the brick through the window and shouted just before your car hit the building," Phoebe said quietly.

"My car hit the building? That's not possible. It was half a block down the street."

"It was, yes. That's where I found it, and I couldn't think of any other way to save your lives, so I, sort of used it for alternative purposes," she said apologetically.

"The motorized light cavalry rides again!" Fred laughed. "Reminds me of when we were sort of pinned down by this Hun machine gun nest, and all of a sudden we heard this rumble behind us and it was some Tommies in an armored Rolls Royce just bristling with machine guns. They put an end to that mischief in a hurry, let me tell you. Miss Phoebe, you took a lesson right out of their play book!"

"I want to see my car," Beatrix said with a grimace. She started to stand up and realized she was light-headed. Both Fred and Harriet helped her to the door.

"Oh my, that does not look good. I do not believe it can be repaired," she said softly. She stared at the crumpled front and broken lights, the shattered windshield, and broken front axle. "That does not look good."

"Doctor Howell, I'm truly sorry. I should have tried to stop Phoebe, but you know how headstrong and willful she can be. We'll pay for it."

"Oh no, dear. Not at all," Beatrix forced a smile through her pain. "It was not a very nice car when I bought it in 1912. It was truly ugly. It is even less stylish now. It's the sort of car an older woman or gentleman would buy. I would have sold it when I bought the Marmon but no one would give me anything for it. Thank you for saving me so much extra work. Now please, help me sit down. The steps will be quite suitable."

"You mean you're not angry with me?" Phoebe asked.

Beatrix forced another smile. "No, not at all. I am very grateful. I believe I would like to sit down."

Horace came out of the flower shop to sit on the front steps next to Beatrix. "You okay, outside of your wrist, that is?" he asked her.

"I think so," she said, then looked away. "Horace, would you check to make sure that your pipe is not broken?"

"Should I take that as a hint?" he asked.

"Yes. I was attempting to be polite."

"It's in my pocket. Same as always."

Phoebe sat down with them, watching as her grandfather lit his pipe. "You know, I've had a pretty rough day, too. Maybe you'll share....?" She asked, nodding toward the pipe.

"No," Horace told her. "Looks like you got here just in time. You know, you saved our lives. I'm fairly certain she would have used that shotgun. Good work. Good clear thinking, young woman."

"Yes, it was," Beatrix added. "Innovative and with initiative. I am surprised you were able to escape without a scratch."

"Well, I jumped out of the car just before it hit the building," Phoebe answered.

"Thunderation! Car! What car? Now, please tell me it wasn't my Franklin," Horace groaned.

"Oh, no. I didn't have the keys for it, and Fred promised to teach me how to hot wire a car, but he hasn't gotten around to that lesson yet, you know, as a battering ram. I used Doctor Howell's Detroit Electric. I'm afraid I wrecked. Looks like I'll be working at the tele-graph office for the rest of my life."

"Beatrix's car? You used her car? I had no idea that old thing could go that fast," Horace said. "Wrecked it, huh? I got to take a look at that! Don't worry about paying for it. I'll do it, and gladly. Between you and me, it was so ugly I hated to be seen in it."

"Me, too, Grandfather," Phoebe answered.

"Truth be told, I was very embarrassed, too." Beatrix said.

Made in the USA
Monee, IL
27 April 2025